Slap Shot!

Three Hockey Stories

D1067162

Slap Shot!

Three Hockey Stories

Irene Punt

cover art by
Jason Laudadio

interior images by
Ramón Perez, Jason Laudadio and Gary O'Brian

Scholastic Canada Ltd.
Toronto New York London Auckland Sydney
Mexico City New Delhi Hong Kong Buenos Aires

Scholastic Canada Ltd.
604 King Street West, Toronto, Ontario M5V 1E1, Canada

Scholastic Inc.
557 Broadway, New York, NY 10012, USA

Scholastic Australia Pty Limited
PO Box 579, Gosford, NSW 2250, Australia

Scholastic New Zealand Limited
Private Bag 94407, Botany, Manukau 2163, New Zealand

Scholastic Children's Books
Euston House, 24 Eversholt Street, London NW1 1DB, UK

www.scholastic.ca

Library and Archives Canada Cataloguing in Publication

Punt, Irene, 1955-
[Novels. Selections]
Slap shot! / Irene Punt ; illustrated by Ramón Pérez and Gary O'Brien.
Contents: The rink rats -- Tryout trouble -- Hockey luck.
ISBN 978-1-4431-7505-0 (softcover)
I. Pérez, Ramón, 1973-, illustrator II. O'Brien, Gary (Gary John),
illustrator III. Punt, Irene, 1955- . Rink rats. IV. Punt, Irene, 1955- . Tryout
trouble. V. Punt, Irene, 1955- . Hockey luck. VI Title.
PS8581.U56A6 2019   jC813'.54   C2018-906333-5

The Rink Rats © 2010 by Irene Punt.
Tryout Trouble © 2014 by Irene Punt.
Hockey Luck © 2015 by Irene Punt.
Illustrations © 2010, 2014 and 2015 by Scholastic Canada Ltd.
All rights reserved.
No part of this publication may be reproduced or stored in a retrieval system,
or transmitted in any form or by any means, electronic, mechanical, recording,
or otherwise, without written permission of the publisher, Scholastic Canada Ltd.,
604 King Street West, Toronto, Ontario M5V 1E1, Canada. In the case of photocopying
or other reprographic copying, a licence must be obtained from Access Copyright
(Canadian Copyright Licensing Agency), www.accesscopyright.ca or 1-800-893-5777.

6 5 4 3 2 1   Printed in Canada 139   19 20 21 22 23

FSC
MIX
Paper from
responsible sources
FSC® C103567
www.fsc.org

Slap Shot!
Contents

*To Tom, Harty and
Heather — with thanks!*
— I. P.

Contents

Rough Ice

"Awesome!"

"Wicked!"

Tom and his friends were inventing hockey plays Sunday afternoon at the outdoor rink at Crescent Park.

The puck passed from Tom to Stuart to Tom to Mark.

THWACK! Mark took a shot on net.

BAM! Jordan punched the puck with his goalie blocker. It rebounded. Tom grabbed the puck with his stick and fired a shot.

"Goal!" he shouted, raising a fist.

Jordan made his scary goalie face and everyone laughed.

"Let's do that passing play one more time!" said Tom. "It's like a pinball machine! *PING PING PING!*"

"Hold it!" announced Stuart excitedly. "Let's call this play The Pinball!"

"Yaah!" Everyone agreed with a high-five. All together they shouted out their hockey team's name — "Glenlake Hawks!"

Jordan grabbed his water bottle and took a big squirt. He lowered his goalie mask. "I'm ready."

Stuart skated backwards. He wobbled and fell. "Not again!" he complained.

Tom looked at the ice. It was rough — full

of bumps, cracks and chunks. His skates and his teeth ch-ch-ch-ch-chattered to the centre of the rink, but he kept his balance. "We gotta do something about this." Then he caught sight of a snow shovel. "You guys keep going. I'm going to start scraping!"

Tom pushed hard on the shovel, thrusting it back and forth across the ice. *SKWYCH! SKWYCH! SKWYCH!* Finally, a stubborn piece of ice broke loose and he flicked it into the snow. "Woo hoo!"

"What are you doing?" asked Stuart.

"Fixing our rink." Tom didn't look up. He grunted, "Unh!" as he grated. *SKWYCH! SKWYCH!* "Yay!" he cheered. "I just flattened the bump Stuart tripped on!"

"Tom thinks he's a Zamboni," whispered Mark.

"Zamboni, baloney!" said Tom, flexing his muscles. "These arms are made to shovel! Watch this . . ." He powered up and worked faster. "Cool!" Another section of ice was smooth.

Mark, Stuart and Jordan stopped skating. Tom seemed to be having more fun than they were.

Stuart positioned his stick next to a lump of crusty snow and joined in. "I'm gonna scrape away this blob!" he said.

"Me too!" said Mark, with a wallop of his stick. "Look! I just got rid of a whopper ice cube!"

Finally, Jordan took off his goalie blocker. "Grrmph!" He revved up.

The boys worked and worked on the ice until . . . *BLEEP! BLEEP!* rang Stuart's walkie-talkie. He pulled it out of his pocket and glanced at his house, across from the park. His mom was at the window, waving her walkie-talkie. "Time to come home!" she told him.

Stuart pressed the talk button. "Hey, Mom. We're kinda busy doing rink improvements!"

"You've got two more minutes!" she said. "Then home!"

"Oh, rats! Let's scrape faster!" said Mark. "This is fun!"

"Rats? Hey, good one, Mark!" Tom laughed. "We're rink rats, like the kids who help out at the arenas!"

Everyone howled.

Five minutes later, Tom studied the rink. It looked bigger. And better. He skated one quick lap, cruised by the net, turned and glided backwards. "Wow! This ice is nice! Check it out!"

The four boys skated back and forth, forward and backwards, while Mark sang, *"Our rink ain't gonna stink no more, no more!"* They raised their hands and slapped a round of high-fives.

BLEEP! BLEEP! Three walkie-talkies blared at the same time.

"Get home, quick!"

"Dinner!"

"You have a game!"

"Uh-oh, it's Game Night! Let's go!" said Tom.

Game Night

Centennial Arena rocked with spectators. Tom strained forward in the players' box, his eyes on the scoreboard. It was now the third period with two minutes remaining. The Woodland Warriors were winning 2–1. *Come on, Hawks! We can do it!* Tom told himself.

Coach Howie rattled the gate for a line change after an icing call. Three tired skaters headed for the bench.

"Mark. Stuart. Tom. You guys are on!"

Coach Howie said, as he tipped his Hawks cap.

"Go, Hawks, go!" yelled the fans.

Mark and Stuart positioned themselves, while Tom set up at the faceoff spot. The linesman dropped the puck. Tom fought for it and lost. As Warrior #2 picked up the pass, Stuart skated hard, reached out his stick and stole the puck. He raced up the ice.

"Pinball," Tom said. "Pinball!"

The puck passed from Stuart to Mark to Tom — over and over as the Warriors goalie shifted up and down, side to side. Then Tom whacked the puck, and it flew into the net.

"The Pinball worked!" Tom whooped.

"Yahoo!" the team howled.

The score was now 2–2.

Again, they set up at centre ice. This time Tom won the faceoff. He tapped the puck to Mark. Mark sent it back to Tom. He caught the pass and took off. *ZOOM!*

The Warriors' winger charged after Tom, swiping at the puck. "Whoops!" cried the winger. His glove and stick went flying. They hit the ice and skimmed across it, blocking Tom's path.

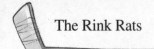

"Oh, no!" gasped the fans.

Tom skate-stepped over the stick. And the glove. His strides were powerful. His eyes stayed focused on the goalie. *THWACK!* He took a shot. The puck soared into the net.

"Yeah!" cheered the Hawks' fans.

"Woo hoo!" shouted the team.

Tom raised his fist as the clock sounded: *BUZZZZ!* The game was over. It was 3–2 for the Hawks.

As Tom lined up to shake hands with the Warriors, he thought, *Skating over obstacles is nothing after shinny on rough ice!*

For the Team

Coach Howie stood in the centre of the dressing room. Fifteen sweaty Hawks sat on the benches around him. "Great game tonight!" he announced. "Tom's fancy footwork was awesome!"

Tom liked his coach. He liked his team. It felt good when he made them happy.

"Now, listen up! I know it's late, but I have an announcement," said Coach Howie. "We weren't able to get an ice time here for our upcoming Family Day game."

"What?"

"Bummer!"

Everyone was disappointed.

"Maybe we could do something different."
Coach Howie looked hopeful. "Any ideas?"

"But playing hockey against our families
is the best!" said Ben.

"How about . . ." blurted Tom, "we have
the game at an outdoor rink?"

Everyone perked up.

"There's one in our neighbourhood that could work," he said, his heart pounding with excitement.

"But most outdoor ice is really bad," said Spencer. "It's like skating on crunchy peanut butter."

Tom signalled his friends for support.

"Hey, no worries," said Mark, spreading his arms. "This rink is smooooooooth!" Stuart and Jordan nodded.

"It's as good as the Saddledome!" Tom added.

"Wow!" Everyone seemed impressed.

"Gee, thanks, boys! This is excellent news!" Coach Howie looked at the team. "I guess the Family Day game is on! Invite the whole gang!"

"YAY!" Everyone cheered till Tom's ears buzzed.

"Now, who wants to help with food, music or decorations? There are lots of jobs to do!" Coach Howie passed around a sign-up sheet.

— ● —

As Tom, Stuart, Mark and Jordan carried their hockey bags down the long hallway,

Mark mumbled, "Oh, man. Our rink's not that good."

"Not as good as the Saddledome!" Stuart gulped. "Yikes!"

"C'mon!" said Tom. "We've got two weeks. We can make the ice perfect."

"What if we can't?" asked Jordan. "The team will be mad at us."

"Hey, we're not going to let a few bumps get in the way of our Family Day game!" said Tom.

"Okay," agreed his friends, banging their fists together.

"We can do this — for the team!" said Tom.

They slapped a round of high-fives, while Mark sang, *"Our rink ain't gonna stink no more, no more!"*

Tom's mom was standing beside the snack bar, talking to Jordan's and Mark's parents. The boys headed in their direction.

"Can we go to Crescent Park right now and work on the ice?" asked Tom.

"No!" the parents answered.

"But . . ."

"But . . ."

"NO!" repeated the parents.

Tom felt deflated. He had been all pumped up and ready to work. He waved goodbye to his friends and headed toward the car as a noisy snowplow scraped the parking lot.

"So, why can't I go to the rink?" Tom asked his mom.

"Because you need to be ready for school tomorrow," she answered.

"Huh?" That's the weirdest reason in the history of the world, Tom thought. He punched his hockey bag into the trunk.

Friendship

Monday, February 1.

Tom sat at his desk, colouring the new calendar page. It was titled *February Fun!*

"Did you know February is the shortest month?" announced Mark.

"Not good!" said Tom. "That means less hockey!"

Mrs. Wong, their teacher, stood at the front of the classroom. "We have a special day in February. Who knows the date?"

Stuart waved his hand. "Friday, February

12th! Everyone's going to wear red to the Calgary Flames game at the Saddledome. They're playing against Sidney Crosby!"

"Go, Flames!" said Mrs. Wong. "But I was thinking of something else."

"Our province has Family Day on February 15th," suggested Tom. "That's when our hockey team is going to play against our families." He looked around at his Hawks friends with a big grin. "I love scoring on my dad!"

"Go, Hawks!" said Mrs. Wong. "But, I was thinking of something else. Here's a clue." She held up a giant red heart. **LOVE** was printed across it.

"Valentine's Day!" said Amber. "February 14th!"

"That's it," said Mrs. Wong. "We'll have a party on the Friday before Valentine's Day — with cupcakes, games and a valentine exchange!" She put a star on the calendar. "Don't forget to wear something red that day!"

The girls smiled and nodded. Jordan rolled his eyes.

"Now, let's start decorating," said Mrs. Wong. She opened a large box and pulled out armfuls of paper doilies, hearts, cupids, roses, and lips. Some of the boys made kissing sounds, and all the girls giggled.

"Yecch!" Tom slid down in his seat. Mark choked. Stuart gagged.

"Oh, dear," said Mrs. Wong. "February

might be the *longest* month." She looked at the decorations. "These things *are* a little sappy. How about no mushy love stuff for Valentine's Day? Instead, let's make *friendship* our theme for February!"

A giant "WHEW!" filled the classroom.

Mrs. Wong continued. "Try making friendship cards for our valentine exchange.

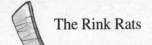

And you can work on a friendship project with your classroom buddies."

Tom looked at his three Hawks teammates. "For our project we can play hockey — and fix the rink!"

Mrs. Wong held up one hand. "The projects must be completed at school and they must demonstrate friendship."

Friendship is easy. February will be a no-brainer, thought Tom.

Shovelling

It was after school.

Tom stomped through a new fall of fluffy snow on the way to Stuart's house. Mark made a giant white puff of breath. "Brrrrr! My nose is frozen." He crossed his eyes to see if it was purple yet. It looked red.

"Grrmph," grumbled Jordan.

They knocked on Stuart's door. His sister, Kaitlyn, answered. "Hi," she said. "What's happening, dudes?"

"We need Stuart to ice-scrape with us," said Tom.

"Ice skate?" asked Kaitlyn. "I like to ice skate!"

"First things first," said Tom, holding up his shovel. "We promised to make our rink good for the Family Day hockey game!"

Stuart came around the side of the house with a shovel. They all tromped across his front yard, making fresh tracks. Mr. Watson,

their neighbour, was slowly clearing his sidewalk. The boys looked at one another. All at the same time, they dropped their hockey equipment and put their shovels to work, up Mr. Watson's driveway and alongside his house, removing the trampled-down snow.

"Wow! You guys plow like the trucks," chuckled Mr. Watson.

"We're just about finished." Tom pushed down extra hard. "Wow! You've got some

stubborn spots!" he said, flipping the shovel blade to the other side to scrape. *SKWYCH! SKWYCH!*

BANG! BANG! Jordan bounced his shovel up and down like a jackhammer to break up the snow.

"I guess I left the snow for too many days and it got packed down solid," said Mr. Watson, red-faced. "Thanks for the help, boys. You saved my sore back."

"No problem!" said Tom. It felt good to help.

Mr. Watson said, "I saw you kids working on the rink yesterday."

"We're fixing the ice — for our hockey team," said Mark.

"You know, if you keep up the shovelling

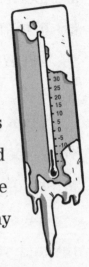

at the rink, I'll help you flood it," said Mr. Watson. "So start watching the weather. Flooding works best on a clear night, when the temperature is between minus ten and minus twenty." He pointed to the outside tap. "You can use water from my house and all my garden hoses."

"Cool!" said Tom, his eyes lighting up. "We'll keep shovelling!"

"We can use water from my house, too," added Stuart.

"I can't wait to watch water freeze!" said Mark.

Mr. Watson chuckled. "When you make it to the NHL, you can tell the fans all about

your days of shovelling and outdoor rinks."
He winked.

"We want to play for the Flames!" said
Tom.

"Then you guys need to get going! Clear
your ice and practise your shots!" said
Mr. Watson.

The boys crossed the street and clomped
through the snow, waving their shovels
in the air, thoughts of playing in the NHL
spurring them on.

"Attack!" shouted Tom, dumping his
stick and skates and tilting his shovel at
the edge of the rink. He pushed hard on the
handle, marching forward with giant steps.
The blade cut through the snow quickly
and easily. Tom stopped and announced,

"Hey, this feels like feathers compared to Mr. Watson's snow!"

"That's because we left the rink in good shape yesterday," said Stuart, zooming along with his shovel.

Ten minutes later, the boys were done and on to hockey — making up a new set of moves called The Pickle Play. An hour later, they sat on the bench, taking off their skates.

"I'm glad we volunteered to fix this ice," said Tom, looking at the rink.

"Ditto," said Mark.

"Ditto," said Stuart.

Jordan nodded.

"It makes me feel like a rink owner," said Tom. "Like this is our rink."

They all laughed.

"We're big-shot rink owners!" said Jordan.

"Hey, let's wear suits and ties on Family Day, like the NHL team owners do!" joked Mark.

Everyone cracked up.

As Tom walked home, he wondered: Should he and his friends play in the NHL? Or should they own an arena? They both seemed like good ideas.

The Friends
of Fred

Tuesday, February 2. Groundhog Day!

Tom sat at the art table, drawing a buck-toothed groundhog on his calendar.

"Psst," said Mark. "What about a Puck Hog Day? For all the hockey players who don't pass the puck!" He laughed at his own joke.

"*Shhh!*" said Mrs. Wong, turning up the radio. "Listen carefully."

The radio announcer boomed, "I'm here with Groundhog Fred at Foothills Farm. When Groundhog Fred came out of his burrow today, he saw his shadow and predicted . . . six more weeks of winter!"

"Six more weeks of outdoor hockey!" added Tom.

Kylie put up her hand. "How can a rodent forecast the weather?"

"Good question," said Mrs. Wong. "Any ideas?"

Mark said, "I think . . . because February is friendship month, Groundhog Fred has *friends* who help him with the prediction — like that radio guy."

"Good answer," said Mrs. Wong, as she signalled the laughter to stop.

"I didn't say anything funny," muttered Mark, blushing.

Suddenly, Tom had a mega brainwave. He caught Stuart, Jordan and Mark's attention. "Hey, let's be Groundhog Fred's friends for our friendship project! Reporting the weather to our class will help everyone — especially the Hawks — because we need to watch the weather for our rink."

"Woo hoo! The four of us will four-cast the weather! Get it?" laughed Mark, holding up four fingers. "The Rink Rats help the rodent!"

A few minutes later, the boys gathered around the science table. Tom studied the five-day weather forecast in the newspaper. "Today is ... mainly cloudy with flurries," he reported. "That means we might need to shovel the snow before our hockey practice."

Stuart checked the outside temperature on the thermometer. "It's zero," he said. "That's freezing. Good for ice. But not cold enough for flooding tonight."

At the end of the day, Mark announced to the class, "The Friends of Fred say: If you get zero on your spelling test, that's bad. But if you want ice, zero is good!"

"Happy shovelling!" added Tom.

Everyone laughed.

The next three days went exactly as predicted: snow, snow, snow, with lots of shovelling, shovelling, shovelling. Each day the temperature dropped two degrees. The Friends of Fred gave these tips to the class:

Wednesday: Minus two degrees — Wear a tuque so you don't freeze your ears off.

Thursday: Minus four degrees — Don't leave your animals outside.

Friday: Minus six degrees — Check the emergency kit in the family car.

— ● —

Saturday. Minus eight and sunny. Game day!

Everyone wore sunglasses on their way to Centennial Arena.

At four o'clock, Tom stood at the spectator glass, watching the Zamboni pass through the gate. He waved at the driver.

"Zamboni, baloney!" hooted Mark, giving Tom a nudge. "Wait till tomorrow when

it's minus ten! We're going to flood our rink like a bird bath!"

"Yaah!" Tom launched himself onto the ice with a powerful stride. *Ooo, this ice seems extra slippery,* he thought, trying to dig in his blades. And when he came in for a stop, his skates kept going. "Oh, no!" he gasped, sliding sideways into the Sunridge

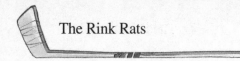

Sharks' team warm-up. *No edges!* But he controlled his knees and held his ankles strong.

The whistle blew. As the team headed for the players' box, Tom said, "We forgot to get our skates sharpened after all that outdoor hockey."

"I guess we're skating on spoons today," sighed Mark.

— ● —

The first period was the hardest. But by the end of the third period, Tom had forgotten all about dull blades. He snatched the puck with his stick and blazed down the rink, while Stuart and Mark criss-crossed the ice to contain the Sharks' defenceman. *BAM!*

Tom took a shot. The puck flew high and hit the glass with a thud.

Spencer tore after the puck, then dug it out of the corner. He popped it to Tom, in perfect position to score. Tom took a swipe, while his feet slipped away from him. He

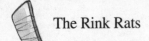

crashed down onto the ice and the puck skimmed right to a Shark.

"Yahoo!" cheered the Sharks fans.

Tom skated hard to the bench, with his head down.

"Shake it off," said Mark. "It's hard to win them all."

Coach Howie tipped his Hawks cap. Tom knew it was his secret way of saying, "Hang in there!"

Flooding

Sunday night. Minus ten!

Tom sat at the dinner table, eating a bowl of hamburger soup. "Wait till you see the rink, Dad!" he said. "It's awesome. We blasted off all the ice chunks, and got rid of the giant piles of snow that were blocking the edges." He visualized the Family Day game. "Our team is going to go crazy!" Tom downed a glass of milk, then stuffed a bun into his mouth.

"Slow down. What's the hurry?" asked Mom.

"Minus ten!" Tom answered. He and Dad gathered up their hockey equipment, boots, hats, gloves and a Thermos filled with hot chocolate. From the garage they got hoses and a nozzle.

———●———

Crescent Park looked vacant. "It's really black at night," said Tom. The only brightness came from a distant street light and the moon. *I'm glad my dad's here*, he thought. Then his eyes adjusted to the dark.

Across the street, Mr. Watson opened his front door. "Something going on out there?"

HONK! HONK! blasted a horn. It was Mark and his dad. Tom waved. Mr. Boswell pulled their equipment bags out of the car.

"We're coming!" hollered Jordan and his older brother, Derek, making their way across the snow.

Stuart plodded to the edge of his yard. "Help!" He looked like a mummy wrapped in garden hoses. "These things are heavy!"

"Whoa!" said Tom's dad. "First the *family* team needs to practise — to get in shape for Family Day. After that, we'll flood the ice."

"Okay," said Stuart, untangling himself from the hoses. "I'll turn off the water."

—●—

The Hawks set up the nets and, a few minutes later, they were circling the rink and making a plan. "Let's show these guys The Pickle Play," said Tom mischievously.

"Good one," whispered Mark. "My dad can't skate backwards."

"Be careful. Remember, Derek's good!" said Tom.

Jordan banged his stick on the pipes. "Let's go!"

Tom placed the puck at centre ice.

"It's hockey night at Crescent Park!" joked Mr. Watson, as he sat down on the bench.

The puck went end to end, was passed and grabbed, over and over. Derek flicked it into the snow bank. "This rink needs boards!" he said, tossing the puck back into the game. Tom batted it down with a slash and a flick. *SWOOSH!* The puck soared into the net, top shelf.

"Yay!" cheered Mr. Watson.

Tom pumped his arm. "Finally!" Now the Hawks had two goals. The family team had three.

BLEEP! BLEEP! Stuart reached for his chest pocket and unzipped the zipper. He pulled out his walkie-talkie. "What?"

"Can I play?" Kaitlyn asked. He looked across the street. She was standing in the driveway, wearing a helmet and a pair of figure skates.

Stuart screwed up his face. "She's pretty bad."

Derek waved his arm in the air. "Kaitlyn … you're on our team! Come on!" Five minutes later, the score was 6–3 for the Hawks.

Tom stopped for a break. "Time to flood the rink?"

"Let's go!" cheered his friends.

As soon as their skates were off, the boys raced over to Stuart's house. But when they reached for the hose, they got a surprise.

"It's frozen solid!" gasped Stuart. There

it sat on the lawn, like a giant pile of rock-hard spaghetti. "Sorry," he sighed. "I forgot about water freezing."

Mr. Watson emerged from his garage, pushing a hose cart. "Here are my garden hoses!" he said. "I've got a hundred metres."

"We brought some hoses, too," said Tom.

They connected them together, and then to the tap. Then they steered the stubborn hose cart across the road and through the snow to the edge of the rink. Stuart stayed back at Mr. Watson's. Tom called him on his walkie-talkie. "Turn on the juice!"

Stuart turned on the tap.

"Yay!" Tom howled. He passed the hose to Mark to Jordan to Kaitlyn to Derek to Stuart — each spraying water onto the ice.

Suddenly a gust of wind whipped over the park, catching the mist and frosting them all. Tom's dad laughed. "You guys look like ice sculptures!" He took a picture with his phone.

As they drank hot chocolate, Tom stared at the rink. It was cool, watching water seep

By the time the hoses were put away, the ice looked as smooth and hard as a hockey helmet.

Wow! thought Tom. *We rule!*

Frustration

Monday. After school.

"Follow me," said Stuart, running toward home.

"Man, why do we have an early practice today?" complained Mark. "I want to skate on *our* rink — right now!"

"I bet the ice looks like glass," said Tom, puffed with excitement.

The boys turned the corner and saw the rink. "AAHHHHH!" they yelled. A bunch of girls was skating on it. Tom's heart was racing as he stomped across the snow. At the edge of the rink he gritted his teeth and took a cold, hard look at the surface. It was covered in scribbles and scratches.

"Hi, dudes," said Kaitlyn, skating up to them. She dug the picks of her figure skates into the ice.

"Uh . . . Kaitlyn . . . what are you doing?" gasped Stuart.

"Practising for Family Day," she said, chopping at a puck with one of her brother's sticks. Her friends skated by, pulling a sled full of Barbie dolls.

Mark choked. Jordan's mouth hung open. Tom was just about to throw his arms in the air and yell, when he saw Stuart's face. "Hey, Kaitlyn," he said instead. "Keep practising. The family team needs all the help it can get!"

Stuart looked up, relieved. "Right on!"

BLEEP! BLEEP! sounded a walkie-talkie. "Get home quick. You have a hockey practice!"

Tom hurried home. He needed to get his skates sharpened.

Centennial Arena.

"Skate backwards! Heads up!" hollered Coach Howie. Tom wove a figure-eight pattern around the orange cones, then glided to a stop behind Mark.

"Are you tired?" asked Mark.

"A little," said Tom.

Mark's face was white. He had dark circles under his eyes.

"I couldn't sleep last night," said Mark. "And I'm still freezing!" He scrambled towards the first cone.

"You're supposed to be skating backwards!" Coach Howie reminded him.

Mark spun around and wiped out. Hard.

Ouch! thought Tom. He skated over to help him up.

Coach Howie blew his whistle. "Okay, Hawks. Get into position for the next drill: The High-Speed Full-Ice Six-Pass Sideways Drill."

"Huh?" Stuart shook his head.

"Passes should be crisp!" added Coach Howie.

"Huh?" Mark frowned. "I don't get it."

Tom shut his eyes, trying to remember everything Coach Howie had said. "It's like we're doing The Pinball." He took a deep, energizing breath. "Let's go."

Tom missed every pass. Mark missed every shot. Stuart missed his turn. And

Jordan couldn't make a save. They were not crisp.

"What's with you guys? You're not even trying!" said Spencer. "This practice is important. Don't you care about the team?"

The words stung. Tom skated slowly to the players' bench and grabbed a water bottle. It wasn't fair. *Wait till they see the rink*, he thought. *We'll show them!*

— ● —

After practice, the dressing room was unusually quiet. Tom unlaced his skates and sat up, his back against the wall.

Coach Howie announced, "Spencer is Team Captain for our next game!" He gave

Spencer a big C to pin on his jersey while Tom held back his frustration.

Coach Howie said, "Team, you looked tired today. You fizzled out at the end. What if it had been a game?"

Mark mumbled, "The Hawks would be dead ducks."

Coach Howie nodded. "Remember, we play against the Tornadoes on Thursday.

They are a strong, fast and smart team." He made eye contact with every player. "How can we prepare?"

"FERP!" said Tom, remembering their secret weapon.

Everyone joined in:

"F — Food!"

"E — Exercise!"

"R — Rest!"

"P — Practice!"

"And BE CAREFUL!" cautioned Coach Howie. "There are lots of bugs going around. Don't share your water bottles!" He looked at Mark. "What's your joke about water bottles?"

"Don't bug me!" everyone shouted.

Except Mark. He muttered, "Oops. I forgot."

Coach Howie finished up with, "We need to stay focused. We're not tweety birds, we are mighty . . ."

"Hawks!" everyone shouted.

Except Mark. He held his throat and squeaked a tiny, "Hawks!"

The boys hauled their hockey bags through the arena doors and headed for the ramp. "No stairs for me," rasped Mark. "I'm outta juice."

"Me too," admitted Tom, still trying to recover from Spencer's jab. "Good thing we've got our shovels to lean on when we fix the rink tonight."

Stuart blushed. "Sorry, man. I'm not allowed out tonight."

Jordan stammered, "I gotta make my

friendship cards for the valentine exchange."

Mark opened his mouth, but nothing came out. He pointed to his throat.

"But . . ." Tom frowned. "We have to stay *focused* — on the rink!" His stomach lumped up like a frozen mitten. *We need to show the team how hard we work!*

You're Not Our Boss

It was Tuesday, after school. Mark was home, sick.

Tom, Stuart and Jordan marched to the rink, shovels over their shoulders, singing, *"Heigh-ho, heigh-ho . . . it's off to work we go!"*

Snow swirled across the ice, blowing around like flying laundry powder. Stuart frowned. "This dry snow is weird!"

They shovelled down the middle of the

rink and around the outside. But when Tom looked up he saw mounds of snow. "What?" he sighed. "This is not working! I'm getting rid of the snow and you guys are putting it back!"

"You mean you're pushing the snow where I've already cleared," said Stuart, being defensive.

"I can't see any ice yet," complained Jordan.

"We need a plan," said Tom, frustrated. He thought hard. "Hey, what about snowplows? They clear at an angle." He positioned his shovel. "C'mon, join on."

Stuart and Jordan lined their shovels up with Tom's. Together they made a giant snowplow-like blade. Together they pushed forward, on an angle. They were almost done when a group of moms and little kids showed up to skate. "I guess we can't play shinny today," sighed Tom.

For a few minutes they watched the little kids charge around the smooth ice, playing happily. They didn't trip on ice chunks. They didn't fall on their faces. Tom felt good about that.

On Wednesday morning, there was a new layer of snow.

After school, Mark came to the rink dressed extra warm. He looked like a woolly marshmallow. "Our friend Fred forecasted winter and he was sooooo right!" he said. A small icicle hung from his runny nose.

Tom ordered, "Okay, guys, use the snowplow method."

Stuart rolled his eyes. "Don't tell us how to shovel. We know."

"No kidding," groaned Jordan, placing his shovel on an angle.

Tom showed Mark what to do.

As the boys pushed forward together,

Tom snapped, "Keep up to the guy next to you!"

"Oh, brother," sighed Mark.

———•———

No one spoke during the game of shinny afterwards. As they were leaving, Tom said, "If it snows again, we'll shovel the rink right after school tomorrow, before our game against the Tornadoes."

"You're not our boss," said Jordan.

"I'm saving myself for the game," said Mark.

"But this rink needs teamwork," said Tom, totally discouraged. "Did you hear the word, work?"

"What's with you?" Stuart stood still.

"Tom, you're forgetting the R in FERP! We need rest for tomorrow's game. We're half-dead."

Why are they acting like this? Tom wondered. *Family Day is a few days away!* Without thinking, he blurted, "Don't you care about the Family Day game?"

"Whaaat?" Their eyes narrowed.

"We're all working hard!"

"Wait, guys!" said Tom, wanting to smooth things over. "You know what I mean."

Mark glared at Tom and mumbled quietly to himself, "Yup, you mean you're being mean."

Tom trudged home, worried about the rink and close to tears.

Fun and Games

Thursday, at school, Mrs. Wong displayed some friendship projects at the back of the classroom. Kylie and Amber made a paper chain, looping together words like Happiness, Laughter, Honesty, Compromise, Magic. Jadie and Taylor made a friendship dictionary. It was opened to KINDNESS.

Tom unrolled his group's poster. It said:

**We FOUR-cast the Weather
with Groundhog Fred!**

The top half was a drawing of the four Hawks, with their hockey sticks and shovels. Underneath, a list of weather tips was printed in felt pen. The latest tip was: **Happy shovelling! Don't let a little bump wreck your day!**

Tom thought about how he really liked being a Rink Rat with his friends. "Hey, guys!" he said. "Let's check out the weekend weather." But Mark, Stuart and Jordan didn't even look up. They stayed at their desks, working on their friendship cards.

"C'mon!" Tom pleaded. They were the only group not working together, and Mrs. Wong was watching. It felt weird — and lonely. He shivered, thinking about yesterday. *Why did I say they didn't care about the rink? Why did I have to be so bossy?*

— ● —

Centennial Arena.

At six o'clock, the Hawks gathered around Jordan for their pre-game cheer. "Hawks! Hawks! Hawks!"

By the second period, the spectators were going crazy. The Tornadoes continued to storm the ice. Again and again their right winger breezed the zones, landing himself a hat trick. Stuart sucked in a deep breath.

Jordan made his scary goalie face.

At 6:45 the score was tied at 3–3. Two players from the Tornadoes sat on their back bench, coughing and sneezing. Their power line was losing its zip.

"Go, Hawks, go!" yelled the Hawks fans.

"Blow, Tornadoes, blow!" yelled their fans.

WHEEE! The ref blew his whistle. The Tornadoes had too many men on the ice.

Bad luck for them, Tom said to himself. Now the Hawks would have a power play — five against four.

Tom said, "Let's try The Pickle." It was Stuart's favourite play.

Tom, Stuart and Mark got into position. The puck dropped at the faceoff circle. Tom batted the puck to Stuart. Stuart jumped at it, scooping the puck onto his blade. The Tornadoes zoomed after him. Too late.

He passed to Tom. Tom grabbed the puck, faked left, spun right and dodged a guy. Instead of shooting, he passed the puck to Mark. Mark flicked the puck as if he

were flicking an ice chunk off his shovel. It whipped over the crouching goalie's head.

"Goal!" the ref called, pointing at the net.

Mark and Stuart celebrated with a glove punch. The score was now 4–3.

———●———

Ten minutes later, the Hawks were singing in their dressing room, *"We are the champions of the rink!"*

Coach Howie looked happy. "That game was a doozy! Great work, Hawks!"

"We just *blew* away the Tornadoes!" joked Mark. "We're not little birds in a windstorm!" He flapped his arms.

Everyone cheered, "We are the Hawks!"

"Don't forget — the Family Day game

is this weekend!" said Coach Howie. "It's going to be a ton of fun!"

Tom gulped nervously, trying to push the rink to the back of his mind.

Jack stood on the bench. "We've got a big-screen TV in our basement and the Flames play tomorrow night at the Saddledome.

Who wants to watch the game at my house?"

"YAY!" The dressing room rocked. Mark and Stuart danced around.

Oh, man. Tom saw how excited his friends were. This was a sweet offer. And saying no would make him a party-pooper. Finally, he said, "Wow! Sidney Crosby! Better get there before the giant snowstorm hits the city!" Then he sat back. He kept a smile on his face, but inside he was worried.

Mark, Stuart and Jordan huddled together. "What about clearing the rink?" they whispered. They looked at Tom for direction. But he didn't look at them and he didn't say anything about it.

Staying Focused

Friday, February 12.

"It's going to be a good Flames game!" said Jordan, on the way to school. "I can't wait!"

"And, look! No snow yet," said Mark.

"Yes. But . . ." Tom's lips twitched. He'd checked the barometer. The storm was on its way.

Stuart said, "Hey, no worries. We have all day Saturday and Sunday to whip the rink into shape."

They walked into the classroom. Everyone was wearing red.

"See?" said Mark. "Everyone is dressed for the Flames game tonight. *Everyone* will be watching it!"

"Go, Flames, go!" cheered Mark, Stuart and Jordan.

"We're wearing red for our Valentine's Day celebration," said Kylie, giggling.

———— ● ————

By lunchtime, snowflakes the size of popcorn were falling. *Oh, no,* thought Tom. He remembered how difficult it was to shovel the trampled-down snow on Mr. Watson's sidewalk. They really needed to shovel today. Not tomorrow. And if the snow was cleared

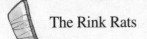

away, they would have a chance to flood the rink before the game — maybe even twice. But Sidney Crosby was playing — their favourite NHL player!

— ● —

Mrs. Wong circled the classroom. She stopped next to the Hawks. They were busy colouring the picture on their friendship poster. "Good brainstorming! Look at all the helpful tips for bad weather!" She smiled. "It's a good thing you boys aren't just fair-weather friends."

"Huh?" The boys shook their heads. Sometimes Mrs. Wong said weird things.

— ● —

Mrs. Wong switched on the happy-face light. "It's party time!" She passed around a tray overflowing with chocolate cupcakes. "Have a snack, open your mailboxes and then we'll play bingo!"

Tom wolfed down his cupcake.

"Psst!" said Mark, with a chocolate smile. He held up the photo Tom had made into a friendship card. It was taken the night they flooded the rink. They looked like ice monsters. The caption said: **To my extremely cool friend — it's snow nice 2 know u!**

Tom opened his mailbox, stuffed with cards. Mark gave him a large flaming letter C. *It's the Calgary Flames C,* thought Tom.

Stuart gave him a postcard covered in scribbles. It said: Thanks for not getting mad at my sister.

Jordan gave him a puzzle card:

Flames @ 6!

"Oh, man." Tom wanted to watch the Flames, but all he could think about were snowflakes falling by the millions. And that made him nervous. *What should I do? Friendship is not easy. It is not a no-brainer.*

Tom looked around the classroom. He liked Mrs. Wong. She said there would be a party and there was. She said "no mushy love stuff" and there wasn't. You could count on her. And you could count on Coach Howie. He always said, "Stay focused and try your best." And he tipped his cap to say, "Hang in there! Never give up!"

Suddenly, Tom knew exactly what to do.

Teamwork

Tom pushed hard on the shovel, lifted a heavy load and dumped it along the edge of the rink. If he multiplied the time it took to clear a short pathway by the amount of snow left, he'd be working till midnight. He took a deep breath and kept going. His friends were probably at Jack's by now.

BLEEP! BLEEP! rang Tom's walkie-talkie. "Turn around!" crackled Stuart.

Stuart, Mark and Jordan were at the edge of the park, waving their shovels in the air.

"Attack!" they shouted, trudging toward the snow-covered rink. The four boys lined up their shovels. "Heave-ho!" They pushed and shovelled down the centre of the rink. They realigned their equipment and made a path around the outside.

Mark sang, *"We're shovelling along, singing our song, side by side!"*

Tom stopped to catch his breath. "At the rate we're going, we'll be finished in time to watch the game!"

"Told ya," said Jordan, "on the puzzle. Flames at 6."

BLEEP! BLEEP! Tom called his mom for a ride to Jack's house, then dug back into the snow. Before long, the rink was a perfect sheet of ice.

"We're done!" shouted Tom. "Just in time!" He held out his fist and everyone banged theirs on top.

"Hawks!" they cheered.

"Wow!" raved Tom, sliding his boots over the surface. "This ice is really nice. The team will love it!"

"Hey, where's your letter C? The one

I gave you at school?" asked Mark. "We voted you Rink Rat Team Captain for the weekend! That's your captain's C!"

"Sometimes we don't mind an extra push, to get the job done," said Stuart.

Tom smiled from his boots up. He saw his mom pull up in the car and Mr. Watson come out of his house to talk to her. "Let's go! Quick! To Jack's house!" Tom said, and they raced across the park.

"Hi, boys!" Mr. Watson stared at their red faces. "I've been noticing how hard you've worked on this rink. You guys have done a great job!" He smiled. "I'm wondering . . . could you check out another rink with me? Right now?" He looked at Tom's mom. "If that's okay with you."

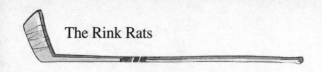

"Oh, sure. Tom loves rink work," said his mom. She smiled. "And the other moms said yes."

Tom glanced at his watch. The Flames game started in twenty minutes. They were doomed.

Flames at 6

The boys slumped in the seats of Mr. Watson's car. Tom sat in front, trying not to frown. They turned left. Headed north. Suddenly, they were in a giant traffic jam. The right-hand lane was bumper to bumper. "Wow," said Tom. "This rink must be really important."

"You betcha," said Mr. Watson, turning into the parking lot of the Saddledome. If it weren't for the seatbelts, the boys would have jumped right through the roof.

Mr. Watson led them to a ticket gate at the main entrance of the arena.

ZIPPP — their tickets were scanned.

"We're really here," said Jordan, pinching himself.

The lobby was buzzing. Nearly everyone was wearing red. "Hurry," said Mr. Watson. "We need to get right down to ice level."

Tom's head spun — taking in the program sellers, the crowd and the Zamboni as they

filed down the stairs. When they were seated next to the ice, Mr. Watson said, "Okay, Rink Rats, tonight you get to watch someone else clean the ice!"

The lights went out.

POOF! Two torches ignited, one above each net.

"Ladies and Gentlemen, your Calgary Flames!" boomed the announcer. A ring of fake fire circled the Saddledome as the

players launched onto the ice. Spotlights zeroed in on their faces as they zoomed into a high-powered skate.

"Ahhhhh!" shrieked Tom, Jordan, Mark and Stuart. "Go, Flames, go!"

BANG! BANG! Harvey the Hound, the Flames' mascot, pounded his drum. "Arrooooo!" he howled.

Then Sidney Crosby stepped onto the ice.

Tom stood up. His jaw dropped and his knees weakened. He pressed his hands on the glass to keep his balance. Then, to his surprise, Sidney Crosby skated right in front of him, his jersey brushing the other side of the glass.

"Oh, man!" Tom gasped, blown away.

"He's awesome!" The players skated into a line and removed their helmets. When the crowd stood and sang "O Canada," Tom and his friends didn't miss a word.

As Tom took his seat, he couldn't help

thinking how much he loved hockey, especially with his friends. A warm feeling tingled inside.

"Now, smile for the camera!" said Mr. Watson, pointing to the TV crew.

Tom and his friends waved.

"Hi, Mom!"

"Hi, Dad!"

"Hi, Hawks!"

Then Tom took a good look at the cameraman's cap. It was the same as Mr. Watson's. He nudged Stuart and pointed.

"Hey!" said Stuart. "I remember. You work for the television station!"

"Well, yes, I do." Mr. Watson winked. "And that gives me some special privileges."

On the way home, Jordan held the game puck in his hands, as if it were made of gold. Mark kissed his Flames ticket. Stuart kissed a photo of the Stanley Cup in his program. Tom hugged his jersey. It was plastered with autographs, including Sidney Crosby's.

Family Day

Monday, February 15. No school. It was Family Day!

Tom opened his front door and grabbed the newspaper. He checked out the weather forecast, then looked at the sky. A mild

chinook wind was blowing through Calgary. It would warm up the day, but not enough to melt the rink into a giant slush drink.

—————•—————

One o'clock. Crescent Park.

As Tom, Stuart and Mark made one final ice check, Jordan set up the nets.

"I can't wait for the opening faceoff!" Tom shouted.

Coach Howie arrived at the rink, carrying

cases of sport drinks. Then the Hawks landed. Jack brought popcorn. Zeke brought a barbecue. Ben brought hotdogs. Kyle and Nat brought music. And Spencer brought a cake that said Happy Family Day!

As the team put up balloons, streamers and a giant Hawks flag, more cars pulled up, spilling out families. They unloaded lawn chairs, blankets, skate bags and hockey gear. Kaitlyn came across the road with Mr. Watson and a new hockey stick. "I'm ready for a hat trick!" she hollered.

After laces got tightened and helmets fastened, everyone gathered at the edge of the ice.

"This rink is great!" boomed Coach Howie.

"Superb job, Rink Rats!" agreed Mr. Watson. He winked at the boys and sat down on the bench.

"Woo hoo!" crowed the Hawks, and everyone clapped.

Tom and his friends leaned on their sticks, smiling proudly.

"Now, let's play hockey!" Coach Howie announced. "Game on!"

*To Dad and Lucy for our many
hours of storytelling.*

— I. P.

Contents

Jitters

"It's going to be a happy hockey day!" announced Tom as he finished his lunch. Tom loved his team, the Glenlake Hawks. He loved playing centre with Mark on right wing, Stuart on defence and Jordan in goal. They were his best friends and they played best . . . together! School and a week of September tryouts were about to start, which made Tom feel anxious and excited at the same time. There was only one thing to do.

Tom grabbed his road hockey stick, gloves and helmet. He headed toward Stuart's house, stickhandling a ball along the sidewalk. *TAP, TAP, TAP . . .*

TAP, TAP, TAP. He turned left. He turned right. He skilfully dodged a light pole. He tried to remember all the things Coach Howie had taught him. Head up. Deke, without losing the ball. Focus. Be positive.

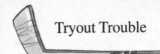

Know the rules. Wear a jock!

When Tom looked ahead, he saw his buddies huddled around the net, waiting for him. "Woo hoo!" they yelled.

Mark was wearing polka-dot board shorts and neon sunglasses.

Stuart was wearing torn elbow pads.

Jordan was wearing his scary goalie face. "Grrmph!" he growled.

Tom ran with the ball, then took a quick shot at the net. The ball hit the crossbar and rebounded to Stuart. Stuart passed to Mark. Mark to Tom. Tom flicked the ball with a wrist shot and it bounced over Jordan's goalie blocker.

"Goal!" shouted Tom.

"Grrr," Jordan growled in frustration. He

scooped the ball out of the net and slapped one to Mark.

Mark controlled the ball and chipped it to Tom. "That was my *gockey* shot. It's like golf + hockey = gockey. Get it?"

Everyone cracked up. Mark was the funniest kid they knew.

Stuart tripped over a pebble as he snuck up behind Tom. He stole the ball, took a slapshot, stumbled and scored! Stuart was the clumsiest kid they knew.

Jordan looked very worried. "Tryouts start this week and my nerves are fr-fr-fried." He slumped over his goalie stick. "I hate tryouts."

"Me, too," said Mark. "We have to compete against each other to get placed on a team.

I say tryouts are *cry-outs*. I've seen the big guys bawl their eyes out."

Stuart covered his ears. "*Shhh!* Stop talking about tryouts! It gives me a rash."

"But. But. What if we don't make the same team?" Jordan frowned.

Tom had never thought of *that*. He and his best friends had been together for two seasons, on the same hockey team and in the same classroom at school. They were a team! They carpooled together. They practised together. They played shinny together. They worked *together*. They were HAWKS! And Coach Howie was *their* coach.

Tom shook his head. Listening to all this tryout nonsense was making a puck-sized lump in his stomach. "C'mon. We'll be together. It's a no-brainer. After all, we are in the same evaluation group!" He held out a gloved fist. Mark, Stuart and Jordan banged their fists on top.

Together they cheered, "HAWKS!"

Now everything was better.

Tom lunged for the ball with his stick. "Let's go!" he shouted. "Keep your head up!"

Mr. Watson's Garage

The road hockey game went on and on and on.

Tom scored six times.

Stuart scored three times for a hat trick.

Mark scored twice.

Jordan lifted his goalie mask and moaned, "Eleven goals! What's with me?" He kicked off his runners and pulled off his orange socks. "Maybe it's these new socks! I remember the last time I wore new socks.

It was when we were playing against the Northland Bulldogs at a tournament. That number 66 scored on me! We lost. And I blew my shutout record!" Jordan made his ugliest goalie face yet.

"Oh, yeah," agreed Mark. "Old, stinky socks are much better."

Tom remembered that game, too. Number 66 was his friend Harty from Champs Hockey Camp a year ago. He had taught Harty his wicked slapshot, and Harty used it to score the winning goal. It was a great hockey moment.

"How about a time out?" hollered Mr. Watson, waving them over to his garage. "I've got slush drinks here!"

The boys put down their road hockey

sticks and raced toward Mr. Watson.
Mr. Watson lived next door to Stuart. He
loved helping the boys with the outdoor
rink during the winter. Today his garage was
filled with big boxes. An old slush machine
was sitting on top of the workbench, next
to packing supplies. He poured
them each a special strawberry
slush.

"Thanks," said Tom, placing
the cold cup on his hot cheek.
"Having your own slush machine is the
coolest."

"No, the coolest thing in the world was
when Mr. Watson drove us to the Saddledome
to see a Calgary Flames game last season!"
said Jordan.

"Oh, yeah!" said Tom, remembering sitting in front row seats.

"Well . . . one day, you guys are going to make the NHL!" Mr. Watson chuckled and winked.

"NHL! NHL! NHL!" chanted the boys as they leapt in the air.

"I will be watching you play when I'm living in sunny Florida," said Mr. Watson. "On my big screen TV."

"What?" gasped Tom. "Are you *moving*?"

Mr. Watson nodded, yes. "'Fraid so. Mrs. Watson is tired of frostbite and wearing long underwear."

Weird, thought Tom, because he loved Calgary and couldn't wait for winter, with temperatures so cold that water froze into ice — and ice turned into outdoor hockey rinks. Tom gulped. He liked Mr. Watson. He had let them use water from his house to flood the outdoor rink across the street at Crescent Park. What would they do now?

As if Mr. Watson had read Tom's mind, he said, "Don't worry about the outdoor rink. I'm leaving behind all my hoses and snow shovels for you boys . . . to keep the rink in tip-top condition!" Then he pointed to the walls, plastered with hockey posters. Some of the posters were autographed by famous players. Others were advertisements for Don Cherry's hockey videos. "I'd love to give you guys all these posters I collected while working at the television station . . ."

"Yes!" gasped the four boys, thrusting

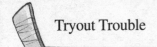

their arms into the air and dancing.

"But . . ." continued Mr. Watson, making the *time out* signal. "I can't."

The boys froze. "Huh?"

"Sorry, boys. We glued the posters to the wall with super-duper extra strength rubber cement. Unfortunately, they must stay in the garage. If I try to remove them, they'll be ripped to shreds."

"Oh, rats," sighed Tom, feeling super-duper extra bummed out. He took a closer look at the posters. "There's the Stanley Cup in Calgary!"

"This poster has all the Olympic goalies," said Jordan in awe. "And their helmets."

"Wayne Gretzky and Sidney Crosby are on the ceiling!" said Stuart, looking up.

Mr. Watson sighed as he cranked up the slush machine and crushed more ice cubes. *GRRR!* It rocked. *GRRR!*

"The people who bought this house scored big time!" Mark told his friends. "I'd sleep in this garage and never shut my eyes."

"No kidding," sighed Tom, checking out the funny Don Cherry posters. He loved watching Don Cherry's hockey highlights and bloopers. Mr. Watson must have collected a gazillion of them.

Mr. Watson took a deep breath. "I am going to miss you guys and the Flames." Suddenly his face lit up. "Hey . . . the new family moves here in a few days. The boy is a real hockey nut. Maybe you'll become friends!"

"No way," whispered Mark. "That kid got all the good posters." He pointed to the slush machine. "I bet he gets that, too. I don't like him already."

As Mr. Watson waved goodbye, he said, "Go Hawks, go! Get yourselves up to speed! And don't forget about school!"

First Day

It was the first day of school, the biggest event of the year!

The schoolyard at Chinook Park School was buzzing with 518 kids looking tanned and shampooed. Tom ran straight to meet Mark, Stuart and Jordan at the monkey bars. It felt good to know where to go and what to do.

Stuart was wearing new runners. They were black, shiny and pinching his heels.

Mark's hair was gelled and spiked. "Do

you like my *scare-do*?" he asked with a laugh.

Tom laughed, too. "Boo!" he said, playing along.

Jordan turned around to show off his backpack. A hawk was printed on the front. Its wings stretched upward and its talons were open, ready for pickup.

"Cool," said Tom. "I think the hawk is grabbing *us* and . . ." Before he finished the sentence, his eyes spied a familiar head of hair in the crowd. It was red and wavy. It was . . . Harty, his friend from Champs Hockey Camp!

"Over here!" Tom yelped, jumping up and waving to him.

"Who's that?" Stuart, Mark and Jordan

chimed. They looked confused.

Tom was too busy flapping his arms to answer. His heart was racing, just like on game day.

The two boys rushed toward each other, greeting with a high-five and a low-five. Harty crossed his arms into a big X. "Give me a high-ten!"

Tom crossed his arms into a big X and did a happy high-ten. "What are *you* doing here?" he asked in amazement.

"We moved to this neighbourhood," answered Harty with a big grin.

"You got a new house?"

"Yup! And . . . a new dad, new dog, new sisters, new grandpa, new cousins, new school . . . and a NEW HOCKEY TEAM to try out for." He looked a little sweaty as he rhymed off his list.

"Wow," said Tom. "I got new school supplies."

"Me, too," laughed Harty.

Suddenly, like a red goal light lighting up, Tom's brain sparked. "Did you guys buy Mr. Watson's house?"

"Yup! The moving truck is there right now."

"Holy moly!" Tom exclaimed. "That makes you Stuart's next door neighbour!" Tom turned to tell his friends . . . when the nine o'clock bell rang. Dr. Dean, the principal, opened the doors to the school.

"Welcome back, children!" she announced from her megaphone, but no one took any notice.

Then, just like last year and the year before, the megaphone sounded off like a screeching cat, "*Kzzkzzkzz!*" It lasted for thirteen seconds, forcing everyone to plug their ears and grimace.

Dr. Dean cleared her throat and came in loud and clear. "Thank you. Now, our teachers have their classroom lists. Please stand beside your grade number and listen for your name." She put on her sunglasses and pointed to the giant signs on the walls.

As the mob ran to hear names, Tom held back. "C'mon!" he motioned to Harty. "Follow me."

"I hope we are in the same class," Harty said, wiping sweat off his forehead.

"Me, too."

Every teacher held a classroom list.

Tom waited and watched and listened for names. He held his crossed fingers in the air as Miss Lucy read her list. Lots of names went right over Tom's head, except, "Mark Boswell . . . Jordan Deerfoot . . . Tom Hiller . . ."

That's me! Go Hawks, go! Tom kept listening and hoping.

"Harty McBey . . ."

Tom's face lit up. *Yeah! Harty's in.* He looked over.

Harty looked happy.

Then Miss Lucy said, "Follow me, class." She flashed a big, friendly smile.

All the students on Miss Lucy's list followed her into the school.

All of Tom's best friends walked toward

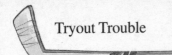

room number seven . . . except Stuart. He was left standing with a sad face, in his pinching, shiny black runners.

Oh, no, thought Tom, looking behind. *Poor Stuart. He's not in Miss Lucy's class this year. And I can't FIX that!* Tom gave Stuart a thumbs-up as he called back to him, "See you at recess! Ball hockey!"

Stuart forced a smile.

Breaking the Ice

Room number seven was colourful and filled with interesting things. Goldfish, a math centre, flashlights, iPads. There were 24 desks, pushed into six groups of four. Tom, Mark, Jordan and Harty raced for the quad closest to the electric pencil sharpener. They set down their school supplies and waited.

"This is my friend Harty from Champs Hockey Camp," said Tom. "We met a year ago."

"You look familiar," Mark said.

"Yes! From Centennial Arena," said Harty. "One time . . ."

Miss Lucy made the *shhh!* sign and waited for silence.

"Welcome to your new classroom!" said Miss Lucy as she wrote her name on the whiteboard. She dotted the letter i with a happy face. "I'm your teacher, Miss Lucy. Together, we are going to have an awesome year! Let's start right now!" She discussed classroom expectations. She handed out more school supply lists. She reviewed the weekly schedule.

Tom looked at the clock. It was only 9:30.

Miss Lucy looked at the clock, too. "Everyone stand up and jog on the spot!"

she said in a perky voice. Her arms swung back and forth.

Suddenly the room was alive with giggles and snorts. *Mrs. Wong never did this!* thought Tom, remembering his old teacher.

Miss Lucy signalled the students to sit. "Now, let's break the ice!" directed Miss Lucy. "Strike up a fun conversation with your group!"

"Did I hear *ice*?" Mark snickered. "C'mon, let's talk hockey!"

"I hate hockey tryouts," said Jordan.

Hmm, thought Tom. *My turn.* He looked at Harty, who was quietly twitching in his seat. "Guess what? Harty's the fastest skater on ice." Tom did a thumbs-up.

Harty's face turned tomato red. "Ahh . . . mostly because I wear stakes, er . . . I mean . . . skates."

"Wait a minute. You *do* look familiar. What team are you on?" asked Mark.

"I used to be a dog," answered Harty.

"Huh?" Mark wrinkled his nose.

"Northland Bulldogs."

Jordan made his ugly goalie face. "Do you know that number 66?"

"Well, yeah," said Harty. "I wa—"

Tom quickly cut him off. "What team now?"

"I am turning into a bird," said Harty. "I am trying out with your Glenlake Hawks."

"Awesome!" Tom slapped a high-five with Harty.

"Tom and I played on the same line at hockey camp," said Harty. "Tom centre, me right wing."

"Wait. Tom and I are on the same line. I am right wing. You can't take my position." Mark wagged his finger.

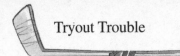

Harty made an embarrassed face.

"Man, oh man. This is why I hate tryouts," said Jordan.

"There are fifteen skaters on a team," Tom reminded everyone. He really liked Harty and wanted his friends to like him, too. What would it take to impress his friends? Suddenly he had a very good idea. "Harty moved into Mr. Watson's house!" he said.

"You got all those good goalie posters," moped Jordan.

"What about the awesome slush machine in the garage?" asked Mark. "We love slushy drinks!"

"My mom said that Mr. Watson didn't leave that slush machine for us," said

Harty. "I think it might be . . ."

Miss Lucy clapped her hands loudly. "Okay, class! Time for more business." She explained the bathroom board. "Don't ask, just write your name on the BB and *GO!*"

"Wow!" said Mark. "Too bad Stuart's not here. He spends a lot of time in the bathroom."

Tom, Mark and Jordan looked at each other, all thinking the same thing. *Stuart, we miss you!*

Finally the recess bell rang and the boys ran out to find Stuart. He was already playing ball hockey with Mario.

"We are in Mr. Sandhu's class," said Stuart.

"Lucky you. My brother had Mr. Sandhu.

He is awesome!" said Mark, doing a spin. "You get to blow up volcanoes in Science!"

"Whoa!" gasped Stuart and Mario, surprised.

Be careful! thought Tom. *When Stuart blows up stuff, he gets blown up, too!*

Tom picked up a stick and reached for the ball. Harty quickly stole it. He passed to Mark. Mark ran with the ball, then tapped it back to Stuart. Harty stole the ball again. This time he flicked it right into the net.

"Woo hoo!" Harty shouted as the bell rang.

It's Just a Game

After school it was hockey tryouts and evaluations at Centennial Arena.

The cold lobby was buzzing with the second group of players and their parents.

"Yikes!" "What dressing room?" "Hurry!" "Where's Coach . . .?" "My mouthguard!" "What time?" "Oh, no!" "I'm stoked!" "We're on!"

They were revved up and ready to be divided into teams.

The big message board read:

NOVICE HAWKS

GROUP B ON NEXT

GOOD LUCK!

Mark rushed through the main arena door with a case of nervous giggles.

Stuart walked slowly, his body covered in blotches.

Harty arrived mumbling to himself.

Jordan dragged a huge goalie bag with his shaking hands. "I hate tryouts," he said to himself.

Tom took no notice of his friends. His stomach felt weird and his head was full of too many hockey tips. *Soft and fast hands. Cradle the puck. Head up. Shoot high. Shoot hard. Anticipate the play.* He trudged past the snack bar, under the bleachers, down the hall and into dressing room number three. Stuart limped alongside him.

"Blisters?" guessed Tom.

"Yeah, I shouldn't have worn new shoes," sighed Stuart, walking on tiptoes. "Now I have to put my skates on and I don't know how I am going to skate."

"Youch!" Tom could almost feel his pain.

—— ● ——

The dressing room was a madhouse as players layered their gear — a jock, shin pads, hockey socks, sock tape, padded pants, skates, shoulder pads, elbow pads, neck guard, practice jersey and a numbered pinny. Then every player snapped on a

helmet, popped in a mouthguard, pulled down a face mask, put on gloves and grabbed his hockey stick.

Coach Howie walked through the door. "Hi, guys!" he said, quieting the room. He took off his Hawks cap.

Tom sat up and listened.

"Welcome back, Hawks! And a warm welcome to our new players. For those of you who don't know me, I am Coach Howie, one of the six coaches running the evaluations. Last year I coached Team Four."

"Yeah!" Everyone from last year's Team Four, including Tom and his friends, cheered.

Coach Howie held up his hand. "The next seven days are going to be crazy. We have over a hundred players to place on six Novice teams. We have three evaluation groups."

Fifteen skaters and two goalies will make a team, thought Tom, doing the math. *Thirty-four in each evaluation group.*

Coach Howie said, "Before you head out onto the ice, in front of the evaluators, I want you to THINK about one big question: WHY? Why do you play minor hockey?"

"NHL!" someone shouted out.

Coach Howie smiled, but didn't respond.

Tom thought about his answer. He loved the game of hockey. He loved playing with his friends. He loved being part of a team. "It's fun!" Tom exclaimed.

"Right on!" said Coach Howie. He taped a Hockey Canada poster to the wall. The

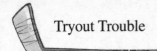

caption read, *RELAX! IT'S JUST A GAME!*

"Now get out there, forget about the evaluators and just try your best!" said Coach Howie.

The door opened.

Mark turned to Stuart, Jordan and Tom. Each boy put out a gloved fist and banged one on top of another, ending with a loud yelp, "Hawks!"

Tom looked at Harty and said, "Let's work extra hard out there, like when we were at Champs Hockey Camp!"

"You're on!" said Harty.

"Here we go!" announced Tom, heading for the freshly flooded ice. A smile spread across his face.

First Evaluation

Tom took long, slow strides while bending and stretching to warm up. The coaches stood at centre ice. The evaluators sat in the stands, holding clipboards and pens. Their eyes followed the skaters as they began gliding around the rink. Tom broke into a swift pace.

A whistle blew. Tom listened.

"Skate forward. We're watching your crossovers," shouted a coach.

As Tom cruised by the scorekeeper's box, Harty passed him and took the corner with ease. *Hmm. Nice.* Seeing that, Tom concentrated. He pushed hard and sped up. He looked into his turn, led with his stick, kept his shoulders up. The toe of his blade hit the ice first as he stepped over and over and over — pushing with his edges. *SWOOSH. SWOOSH.* He took the corner beautifully. His crossovers were nearly perfect.

"Faster!" shouted a coach.

Tom looked ahead. He caught a glimpse of Mark. His left shoulder drooped and his skates were hitting the ice heel first.

OH, NO! thought Tom.

"Now skate backwards!" hollered a coach.

Determined, Tom pivoted and turned.

Stuart tripped over his feet and thumped bum-first into the boards. Twice.

OH, NO! thought Tom.

Jordan crouched between the pipes as a goalie coach took shots on net. Jordan swatted the flying pucks with his big goalie

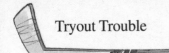

stick. "Grrmph!" he growled, making his scary goalie face. Four pucks swirled around his feet.

OH, NO! thought Tom.

— ● —

"Everyone against the boards," ordered Coach Howie. "Quick stops and starts across the ice! Four times!"

"Faster!"

"Now back to the boards!"

The coaches skated past the skaters, taking note of who was tired and winded.

Tom felt great, but some skaters were red-faced, slouched and gasping for air. He checked out his friends. They all looked good following *this* drill. Summer road hockey had paid off for them.

The evaluation moved on to stick-handling, passing and shooting. The last fifteen minutes were game time.

Little reminders kept popping into Tom's head. *Look where you're passing. Soft hands. Don't shoot at the goalie. Follow the shot for a rebound.*

Tom glanced up at the stands. The evaluators barely smiled as they took notes. Tom decided to stop worrying about them and keep trying his best. It was just too hard to worry and work at the same time.

On Tom's last shift he won the killer faceoff. He blazed down the ice, steering the puck toward the net. He passed to Mark — Mark to Harty — Harty to Tom.

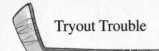

He caught the puck, swooped in front of the net and scored! *YES!* Tom felt pumped.

At the end of the hour, the buzzer sounded and everyone cleared the ice for the next group of skaters — Group A.

— ● —

Back in the dressing room, Mark was squirting his water bottle over his head.

"That evaluation was a doozy! I don't feel like a Hawk any more. I feel like a dead duck!" He laughed at his own joke.

Stuart was close to tears. "My feet. My feet. Ooh-aah." He unlaced his skates and carefully pulled them off.

Jordan looked happy. "I was good . . . 'cause I wore my oldest and stinkiest socks."

I feel pretty good, too, thought Tom. *I kept my head up. I focused. I showed them my wicked slapshot.* He smiled.

"Hey, guys!" Mark called out. "Who knows this one?" He held up his pointer finger and the song broke loose.

> *One, two, three, four,*
> *C'mon Hawks, shoot and score!*
> *Five, six, seven, eight,*
> *We are Hawks, we are great!*

One, two, three, four,

C'mon Hawks, score some more!

Five, six, seven, eight,

Win those games, we can't wait!

"Go Hawks, go!" howled Mark, flapping his arms and wiggling his bottom.

Harty sat off to the side, not knowing the cheer and looking awkward. He tore the sock tape off his socks and layered it onto the giant tape-ball he kept in his hockey bag. He seemed sad.

Tom looked at Harty.

"Whoa!" Tom interrupted everyone. "Check out Harty's monster tape-ball! I bet it weighs a hundred kilos!" He picked it up with a fake struggle. "Umph!"

"Let me try!" "Let me see!" "I'm next!" said the group.

"I've got two seasons . . . or . . . over fifty games of sock tape in this ball," Harty said, proudly. "From when I played for the . . ." He stopped before saying, *Northland Bulldogs.* He looked around. Everyone was a happy Glenlake Hawk. He wanted to be one, too.

Band-Aid Buddies

Coach Howie entered the dressing room carrying a case of sports drinks. "Here, guys. Free samples of Grape Guzzle! I got them from work." Coach Howie was always bringing in samples from the Smokin' Cola Company. Mark piped up, reciting the TV commercial: "Great Grape Guzzle! is so DELICIOUS, it's RIDICULOUS!" *BURP!*

Everyone laughed. Mark took a bow.

"Enough, Mark," said Coach Howie.

He looked tired. "Here's what's next. Go home and sleep. You will receive an email tomorrow telling you what time your next evaluation is. Don't be alarmed if you are asked to join Group A or C. Don't think of it as being moved up or down. Just think of it as being moved *around*. The coaches and evaluators are trying their best to place you on a team where you will play the most hockey . . . and have the most fun! See you in two days."

One by one, players exited the dressing room looking pooped. Jordan and Mark gave a salute as they left to catch their rides.

Stuart sat on the bench, nearly a zombie. "First day of school: not so good. First day

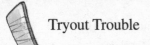

of tryouts: not so good. First day wearing new shoes: BAD IDEA!"

As Tom struggled to unknot his skate laces, he told Stuart what his grandma always said: "Things will get better. And tomorrow will be a better day."

"Yeah, right." Stuart huffed and rolled his eyes. "Easy for you to say."

"Wait a minute!" Harty reached into his hockey bag. "Here. Want these?" He held out

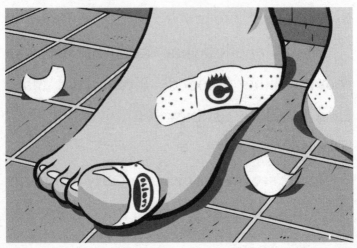

a box of Band-Aids. They had NHL team logos printed on them.

Stuart's eyes widened. "Wowzers! I love these!" He peeled them open and stuck the Calgary Flames on his biggest blister. The Edmonton Oilers went around his big toe. The Toronto Maple Leafs covered his left heel.

"They work best when you double them up," instructed Harty.

"You get blisters, too?" Stuart asked.

"Yup. Big, juicy ones that pop water and then look like strawberries." Harty frowned.

"Whoa!" said Stuart. "We could be blister buddies."

"Oh, yeah!" laughed Harty, his face lighting up. He removed his socks and showed

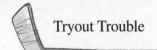

Stuart a scar shaped like a mouthguard.

Stuart clapped. "That's a keeper."

"I'm going to *love* being your neighbour!" said Harty. "We can walk to school together."

"Yes!" said Stuart, jumping up. He bumped his head. "Ouch! At least I have Band-Aids so I can walk again."

Tom watched Stuart and Harty, happily Band-Aiding. *Hmm. I'm usually the one making Stuart feel better.*

Harty and Stuart did a high-five and a low-five. Then Harty made an X with his arms. "C'mon Stu! Give me a high-ten!" he said.

Tom's heart sank. He had never been jealous of scrapes, scabs, blisters, bumps, bruises and Band-Aids before. But he was today.

Two Day

Tom walked slowly to school. Every muscle in his body ached. He scrunched his shoulders. His backpack felt like he was piggybacking a hippopotamus.

He saw Harty, hanging out with Jordan, by the swings. They were practising their scary faces.

Jordan did his usual scary goalie face. "Grrmph!"

"You look amazing!" complimented Harty. "Now try this one." He wrinkled his forehead, gnashed his teeth and snarled like a raging pit bull, "Garrrrgh!"

"Good one!" said Jordan. He concentrated. He copied Harty's ugly face and did a much bigger growl. "GarrAWWW!"

Harty shook his whole body and chattered his teeth. "See how scared I am? Your look is NHL material!"

Tom couldn't help frowning. He had never been jealous of Jordan's ugly face before, but he was now.

"Jordan, I have an idea!" said Harty. "You would look fearless if you drew fangs on your goalie helmet." He reached into his backpack and pulled out his new felt markers. "I can help you. And if you come over to my garage we can check out the NHL posters for ideas."

Jordan's face went from ugly to super happy. "Yes! Yes! Yes!" He jumped from one foot to the other, his arms flailing in the air. "You are the best! I think my hockey tryout jitters are gone!"

Tom stood by watching. He felt invisible to Jordan and Harty. *Hmm*, Tom thought.

I'm usually the one teaching stuff to Jordan. Harty was starting to bug him — big time.

———●———

The bell rang and the playground emptied as students streamed into the school.

Miss Lucy swung door number seven open.

"Good morning, class! Welcome to day number two!" Her hair was in two pigtails, and she was wearing two name tags, two watches and two pairs of glasses. "Find your seats."

The desks were pushed into twos. Mark

and Harty were a pair. Jordan and Raj were, too. Tom found his desk. He was Kylie's partner. She was wearing pink butterflies in her hair.

"Today we are learning about words that are spelled the same but have two completely different meanings," said Miss Lucy. "They are called *homographs*."

"Like the word . . . *rose*?" Kylie asked eagerly. "I *rose* from my soft purple chair. And a yellow *rose* is a beautiful flower."

"Yes! Exactly! See how many you can think of with your partner," said Miss Lucy. "I have a surprise for the winners!"

Immediately, Kylie began to make a list. She was like a homograph machine, spitting out *fly*, *rock*, *pop*, *duck*, *boot*, *bat*, *tip*, *bank*, *ball, sock*. She looked at Tom. "C'mon, think! Two brains are better than one!"

"Stick," offered Tom.

"Is hockey the *only* thing you think about?" asked Kylie. "Hockey, hockey, hockey."

"Pretty much," said Tom. He looked over at Mark and Harty. They were having two hundred times more fun with homographs.

"*Toot*," joked Mark. "*Toot* sounds like a two word! The train *toots*. And I *toot* after eating chili!"

Mark and Harty cracked up.

"*Sport!*" howled Mark, with tears running down his cheeks. "You are a good *sport*. And we play a *sport* — HOCKEY!"

Hmm, thought Tom. *I am usually the*

one joking around with Mark and helping his punchlines. But today, Tom felt like the boring guy.

"Mark, do you want to watch some Don Cherry videos at my house?" said Harty. "The bloopers are the funniest hockey moves in history."

Tom's heart sank to his runners. *I wanted my friends to like Harty . . . but not more than they like me!*

"Hey, Tom. We need more words," said Kylie, snapping her fingers.

"*Puff!*" said Tom. He thought, *I am watching Mark* puff *up. And in a* puff, *my Hawks are off — without me.*

"Puff is a nice word," agreed Kylie, and she added it to the list.

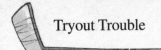
Tom sniffed back a secret tear.

As Kylie worked on their list, Tom wrote his name on the BB and left the class. Maybe he would see Stuart in the bathroom. He'd have a tissue.

A New Cookie

Tom trudged home, alone and grumpy. He headed directly for his backyard.

A practice stick and pucks were scattered on the walk. Giant truck tires leaned against the brick wall. Tom grabbed his stick and took a few shots at the tire targets. *Bang! Bang! Bang!* Right into the centre of the tires.

Rap! Rap! Rap! Dad knocked on the kitchen window. "Hey, Tom!"

"Hi, Dad!" yelled Tom. "Did you get an email with my evaluation time?"

"No, not yet." shouted his dad.

"No?" Tom headed for the kitchen. Dad was shuffling cookies from the oven to a cooling rack.

"Hey," said Dad, looking up. "What's up? What did you learn at school today?"

"Number two," answered Tom.

"Number two?" Dad had a crooked smile on his face.

"Yeah. We did number two." Tom rolled his eyes and grinned. "That's when Kylie and I won the word contest prize. We get to feed the goldfish twice this week."

"Awesome!" said Dad with a high-five.

Yeah, thought Tom. *It feels good to win. Kylie was a pretty good partner after all. She really challenged me.* He grabbed a cookie. "Huh?" Tom looked carefully. It was brown with slimy green bits.

"I just invented the chocolate dill pickle cookie," said Dad, proudly. "C'mon, try it . . . a new mix. You love chocolate and dill pickles. Why not together?"

"Okay." Tom liked the way his dad did crazy things. He closed his eyes and bit into the gooey, warm cookie. It felt weird in his mouth and tasted a little odd. He tried another bite. "You know . . . the more I eat, the better it gets." Tom smiled and reached for another cookie. "Mmm. These could become my new favourite cookies! Maybe even the *world's best!*"

"*Shhh!* Don't tell your mom that! She'll be hurt and jealous."

"What? That's crazy," said Tom.

"Well, nobody likes to feel replaced. And Mom fancies herself the cookie boss here." Dad winked.

Tom thought back. He had felt replaced all day and it didn't feel so good. "Would Mom be mad if I liked *both* of your cookies? Like a tied game with no winner or loser?"

"I think that would be perfectly fine,"

said Dad. "After all, there is room for two good cookies in the world. And a little competition makes you try harder."

Tom downed a glass of milk. *RRRING!* He jumped to answer the phone. It was Jordan looking for a ride to the next Group B evaluation at four o'clock the following day. "I hate tryouts," he reminded Tom.

RRRING! Mark was in Group B.

RRRING! Stuart was in Group C at six o'clock!

"Oh, no," Tom told Dad. "This is not good. What if we are not on the same team this season?"

"Well, it could happen," said Dad. "There are lots of players moving up a division. The coaches and evaluators have a big

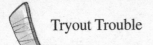

job placing players. Most of them have the exact same skills."

Tom held the phone in his hand, waiting for more calls.

Ding! Ding! The computer chimed with a new email from Glenlake Hockey. Tom opened the email and read:

> **You are now in the Novice**
> **Group A evaluation.**
> **Centennial Arena tomorrow**
> **at 5 o'clock.**

Tom panicked. "I'm in the A group! That's usually the Team One and Two group! I have always played on a Team Four!"

"You have worked hard," said Dad. "You are a good team player. You take the game seriously. You play with heart. So I think you are ready for the challenge."

Tom felt like he had swallowed a puck. This news felt good and scary at the same time. *Teams One and Two! Wowzers! But . . . but . . .* "What if I totally mess up?"

"Thomas Hiller! You give it your best shot. And remember . . . anyone can have a blooper!" said Dad.

RRRING! It was Harty. He was in Group A, too. And he was trying out for the same position as Tom, CENTRE.

Team Players

Centennial Arena. Four thirty. Novice tryouts.

Tom stood by the spectator glass watching Group B battle for the puck in a fast-moving game. Jordan was in goal. Mark was right wing. They were on opposing teams — red pinnies versus green pinnies.

Mark caught a pass from his green defenceman. He guided the puck along the boards then crossed the ice. He passed to his centre.

Jordan skated forward, shifting his stick to a blocking position. He made his ugly goalie face with his eyes glued to the puck. "Grrmph!"

THWAP! Jordan stopped the first shot. Mark caught the rebound and circled back, gaining control. *THWAP!* Mark's shot was crisp. But Jordan stopped the puck again, this time with his glove. The puck slid to Jordan's red defenceman. He passed it to open ice.

Bad play on defence, thought Tom.

Mark raced for the puck, picked it up on the end of his stick and took a giant slapshot. *PING!* The puck soared over Jordan's shoulder . . . into the net!

"Yahoo!" Mark cheered, holding his stick above his head.

"Way to go, Mark!" shouted Tom.

"Way to go, Mark!" echoed Harty. "You are awesome! Hang in there, Jordan! You rock!"

Mark and Jordan looked over and smiled.

Oh, boy. Here we go again! thought Tom. It had been another long day at school with Harty stealing his friends. Harty burped the longest burp with Mark. Harty drew the scariest picture with Jordan. Harty got the blackest bruise with Stuart. And Harty won the Day Three three-letter-word competition with Kylie. Tom shook his head. *Will this guy ever stop?*

"Hey, Tom," Harty whispered. "Are you ready for Goop A? Er . . . I mean Group A?"

Tom ignored him. He watched more hockey.

Harty shrugged and frowned. "I really miss my old friends and Bulldogs. My life *was* easy peasy, and now everything is new." He took a deep breath. "Including Mark, Jordan and Stuart."

Tom was not ready to speak.

Harty pushed on. "Thanks for sharing all your friends with me. I was super freaked out about moving to Chinook Park. But you made it easy for me." Harty tapped his  stick. "Mr. Watson was right."

After the longest silence ever, Tom raised an eyebrow and asked, "What did Mr. Watson say?"

"That you guys are the best. That you have more fun than a barrel of monkeys. That you look after each other," said Harty. "You are team players through and through."

Tom blushed. Mr. Watson's words had stung. *Being a team player is the most important thing. It means being unselfish, sharing, trying your best. Oh, boy.* Tom felt guilty. He had not been the best to Harty just now. *Why is sharing your best friends so difficult?*

Harty continued, "Mr. Watson also said that I am to share all the old hockey stuff he left in the garage. He gave me a heads-up on what you guys would like: pads for Stuart, NHL stuff for Jordan, funny videos for Mark. Next time you get a drive over, you get the

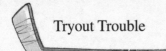

slush drink machine. Mr. Watson said that you would know exactly what to do with it."

"Whoa! Me? I get my own slush machine!" exclaimed Tom. "Mr. Watson is so cool, he's frozen!"

Tom looked at Harty, who had tried his best — all week, in every way. "I'm glad you moved to Chinook Park. You are like a new cookie. Different, but good."

"Huh?" Harty laughed.

Tom crossed his arms into an X and they clapped a high-ten.

Group A

Soon the arena was buzzing with more players. Tom didn't recognize anyone.

"I'm so nervous for the Group A evaluation. What about you?" whispered Harty.

"Me, too," said Tom, his stomach knotted. "It's scary."

"Do you think we could both be centres on the same team?" asked Harty.

Tom thought about it. There is only one centre per line. But every team has three lines. It *would* be nice to have Harty on his team. "Anything is possible," said Tom. Suddenly he felt better thinking they'd be together.

"Hi, guys!" It was Coach Howie. He was holding a large case of Lucky Lemon Guzzle. "Here, take one of these drinks for after your evaluation. Now you'd better get going. Suit up for Group A!" Coach Howie looked proud as he patted them on their backs.

"What if we both make Team One?" asked Harty.

"Ahh!" gasped Tom, choking. He opened his drink and guzzled it back all at once.

Harty did the same thing. Then together they let out the biggest *BURRRP!*

———●———

At five o'clock the new evaluators studied Group A. They were on the lookout for forehand, backhand, tape-to-tape passes, position, puck control, speed, strength, endurance, attitude, effort and sportsmanship.

At 5:30 everyone stopped for a water break. Tom finished off his water bottle and got it refilled. So did Harty.

"Whoa! Holy smokes," Tom told Harty. "Group A is way faster than Group B. Everything is electric! The passes, skating, plays, coaches' calls . . ."

"I sure don't feel like the fastest skater any more!" admitted Harty. "But I am pushing myself hard."

"Me, too," said Tom. He took another gulp of water.

They headed to the bench, ready to play a fifteen-minute game. Purple pinnies against white pinnies. Tom and Harty wore purple ones.

On Tom's first shift, he missed the faceoff.

On the second shift, Tom won the faceoff. He slapped the puck back to the defenceman and charged for the blue line. *OH, NO! He shouldn't be there!* The puck was turned over to the white pinnies. Their left winger passed to his centre. The centre barrelled down the ice in a breakaway, took a shot, SCORED!

Back on the bench, the coach said, "Tom and Harty, next shift I'm going to put you guys together, as wingers. Tom left wing. Harty right wing."

"Okay," they said.

"Weird," whispered Tom.

On the third shift, Tom and Harty filed onto the ice. Tom grabbed the puck. He faked left and went right for a perfect deke. Tom looked to Harty for a pass. Harty's head was out of position. One shoulder was dropped. He was slightly bent over and his knees were knocking together. A white pinny was closing in on Tom. Tom passed to his defenceman. The puck came back to Tom.

Suddenly Tom realized what was wrong with Harty. He had to go pee! Tom skated back down the ice and . . . oh, no . . . it hit him. Tom had to go, too! Youch! He couldn't balance and his knees started knocking together. His skating went from long, smooth strides to little baby steps with his heels.

His crossovers were over.

Harty was now in worse shape. His face purpled, just like his pinny.

Together they got out of the play and off the ice.

———●———

Back in the dressing room, Tom sat on the bench like a deflated balloon. Noise and laughter circled around him.

"I guess we are the Purple Pee Guys," Harty whispered with a crooked smile.

Tom brightened. "A couple of big bloopers," he whispered back. "Drinking that Lucky Lemon Guzzle before our evaluation was *bad* luck!"

They both laughed.

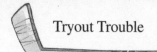

"We will never forget today," they said together. "Jinx!"

Coach Alex entered the dressing room. "Hi, guys!" he said, quieting the room. "You have one more evaluation and then you are on your team! Check your email! Now, go home and get rested up." He set down a case of Lucky Lemon Guzzle by the door. "Grab a refreshment on your way out! Courtesy of Coach Howie!"

When Tom reached the long hallway, he spied Stuart, dressed and ready for the Group C evaluation. His face was covered in blotches and he was wearing enormous shoulder pads.

"You look like serious defence!" complimented Tom.

"Thanks!" Stuart beamed. "And those NHL Band-Aids make my feet feel great. I'm ready! Bring it on!"

"Yeah! Good luck out there!" Tom and Harty told him. They swigged back their drinks.

"Thanks," said Stuart. He frowned. "Lucky you guys. You got a drink! It took me so long to get my gear and Band-Aids on, I missed out! It's not fair. Everyone in Group C guzzled a Guzzle, but me!"

"Whoops," said Harty. "You might be the lucky one. I have a feeling that you are going to ace this evaluation!"

Tom looked up into the stands where

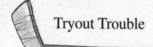

the evaluators were taking notes. *I wonder which team or teams we will all end up on.*

"Hey, Stu ... just try your best!" Tom said.

Team Photos

Finally a week of tryouts was O-V-E-R!

Tom sat on a stool in his kitchen, with new school supplies, finishing homework. He was to write about his week as if he was a news reporter. He sharpened his hockey stick pencil and wrote the hockey highlights first.

Stuart Vickers looked like a hockey pro in Group C!

Mark Boswell and Jordan Deerfoot were solid players in Group B!

Harty McBey and Tom Hiller were bloopered out of Group A!

Coach Howie returns to coach!
There is a new cookie in town!

Mom placed a cold glass of milk and a plate of Raisin Bran cookies in front of Tom. "I am glad this week is over," she said. "Now we can get on with a fun season. I hate tryouts."

— ● —

Six o'clock. Centennial Arena was buzzing. All six Glenlake Novice teams were dressed in gear and ready for their team photos.

Coach Howie held a megaphone. "Congratulations, Hawks! A new season is about to begin!" Then, just like last year and

the year before, the megaphone sounded off like a screeching cat, "*Kzzkzzkzz!*" Everyone plugged their ears and grimaced. Finally Coach Howie came in loud and clear. "Now . . . please stand with your coach and your team."

Tom stood with his teammates, huddled around their coach, Coach Howie. Besides him, there was Harty, Mark, Jordan, Stuart and twelve more. *They* were officially Team Three. "Woo hoo!" they hooted.

Tom glanced at his four best friends.

Mark looked happy, as if he'd just told a zinger of a joke.

Stuart's blotches were gone.

Harty blabbed with everyone about everything. His words were fast. "New

Hawks new house new sisters new hockey new school new dog new skates . . ."

Jordan made his happy goalie face. "Tryouts were okay," he mumbled.

Tom felt proud wearing his new Glenlake Hawks jersey. *Tryout troubles are over*, he thought. *Today is a better day!*

The photographer motioned where to go.

As the five boys moved into their positions on the chairs, Coach Howie said, "Smile for the camera! Don't worry about your hair! We're not peacocks, we're HAWKS!"

Everyone laughed.

"Click!" The photographer snapped a photo. It was just about perfect. Except . . . Mark's jersey was inside out, Stuart sneezed, Jordan looked down, Harty's mouth was

open and Tom's mind was wandering. He was having visions of winning Calgary Minor Hockey Week and even the City Championships . . . this year for sure! Suddenly he was blasted out of his daze when Coach Howie announced, "Okay, team, we've got twenty minutes of ice time! Let's get out there and scrimmage! Get those new jerseys stinky!"

"Let's go!" shouted the team.

Team Three scrambled through the gate onto the ice. The two goalies set up in net. The fifteen skaters took turns playing out. The puck zoomed end to end. Players passed, passed, passed to their teammates. *I love hockey! I love being a Hawk!* thought Tom, with a warm feeling inside.

Finally Tom, Harty, Stuart, Mark and Jordan ended up on the ice at the same time. They set up: Jordan in goal, Tom at centre, Harty and Mark wingers, Stuart on defence.

Tom won the tricky faceoff. He shot the puck back to Stuart. Stuart grabbed the puck and knocked it along the boards. Mark picked up the puck and passed it to Harty. Harty to Tom. Tom back to Harty. Harty blazed down the ice on a breakaway. He wound up and blasted a wicked slapshot . . . right into the net.

"Yippee!" yelled Tom, followed by, "Oh, no!"

Everyone ended up in a dog pile in the net.

They picked themselves up and gave a quick group hug. They pumped their arms and raised their sticks while skating back to the bench. When Tom looked through the spectator glass, he saw Harty's family. They were cheering like crazy. It was the cheer Mark sang in the dressing room.

One, two, three, four,
C'mon Hawks, shoot and score!
Five, six, seven, eight,
We are Hawks, we are great!
One, two, three, four,
C'mon Hawks, score some more!
Five, six, seven, eight,
Win those games, we can't wait!
GO HAWKS, GO!

Suddenly Tom knew exactly what to do with the slush machine from

Mr. Watson . . . have a "Welcome to Chinook Park" party for Harty's family. He began to think. *Maybe in Harty's garage! With the NHL players all around. After all, the more hockey, the better!*

*For Jackie Bevis. I'm lucky
to have such a good friend.*

— I. P.

Contents

Hawks' Luck

Tom sat on the wooden bench in the dressing room at Centennial Arena. His hair was wet. His throat was dry. His face was hot. His feet were cold. "I love hockey!" he announced, slapping high-fives with his best friends, Stuart, Mark, Jordan and Harty. "What a game!"

"Yup! It's a fun day Sunday! We put two eggs in the nest!" said Mark. He flapped his arms and squawked, *"Tweet, tweet!"*

Everyone cracked up.

I love being a Hawk, thought Tom. It was his third year playing hockey on the Glenlake Hawks. This season he and his friends moved up to the Novice Three team. Coach Howie was their coach. Yellow and green were their team colours.

Tom gazed around at his teammates. Everyone was smiling. Everyone had a wet "sweat head." It was early October and the start of a new season, but some things never changed. And that felt good. Only one thing could have made the game better for Tom . . . getting his first goal of the season.

"*PSST.* We won our game because I stuck NHL Band-Aids on my blisters," said Stuart proudly. "They always bring me good luck." He flashed a toothy smile.

"I eat lucky pizza on game day," said Mark. "Because a pizza that's cheesy makes scoring easy!" He reached into his hockey bag and found a slice of pepperoni pizza left over from breakfast. "I am not joking, guys. If I eat pizza, I get a goal. It's like magic!"

"I get dressed in a special order for good luck," added Harty. He explained his routine: "I put on my elbow pads first, jock second

and gloves last. Then, I tuck the left side of my jersey into my hockey pants — just like Wayne Gretzky did."

"Nope," Jordan shook his head. "We won because I wore my stinkiest socks. I hide them in my goalie helmet so they never get washed." He pulled off his goalie skates. "Smell these! Once they were white and now they are bluish grey brown!"

Tom listened to his friends talk about their hockey superstitions and good luck charms. Without his lucky number 15 jersey, he needed to tell himself, *These guys are crazy. Good luck stuff is silly. There is no such thing as HOCKEY LUCK!*

Everyone in the room was showing off their weird ideas about luck. "I sing "Happy Birthday" when I tighten my skates." "I wear red underwear." "I pinch myself before going on the ice." "One time I ate three mini pizzas and got a hat trick!"

"Oh, NO!" Suddenly, Mark leapt across the room to where the hockey sticks were propped up in the corner. "TOUCH WOOD!" he called out. "Quick! Knock on wood! Before you jinx your good luck by bragging about it!"

The team followed Mark's instructions because nobody wanted to jinx their luck. "Touch wood!" they chorused, knocking on the bench, and knocking on their heads. *RAP! RAP! RAP!* Tom shut his eyes. Deep down, he respected hockey superstitions. He knew good luck charms were important. Lots of players in the NHL had them. *When you own something lucky, you remember all the times it brought you good hockey luck. And when you own something unlucky* . . . His heart sank. Tom pulled off his new home jersey — number 5. He frowned at the problem and stuffed it into his hockey bag.

Number 5

Coach Howie entered the dressing room. "Hawks, you are the luckiest team on the planet!" he announced. "I've never seen anything like it. Tied at 1–1 in the last minute of the game and the goalie sneezes just as Mark takes a shot!" Coach Howie wiped his forehead. "Good thing I wore my lucky cap!"

Mark looked smug. "I say . . . pizza with cheese made the toughest goalie in the league . . . sneeze! And I got a goal!"

"We *are* on a lucky streak. Remember last week? We won when the Sharks scored on their own goalie!" Jordan grinned. "It was like winning the lottery!"

"And what about that crazy bounce off the top of the net?" asked Harty. "We *blooped* and . . . we scored!"

The room exploded with laughter.

Coach Howie stood on the bench. "Okay, Hawks. Settle down! I'm worried our luck will run out. We can't count on fluky goals to win! Let's get back to the basics of good hockey: using skills and executing plays." He clapped and gave a thumbs-up. "Great win today! Our next game is Wednesday at 6:30."

Mark winked at his friends as if to say, "No worries, my luck is golden. We can count on pizza!"

Tom looked like a melting snowman. His arms drooped and his head hung low. He liked Coach Howie and, more than anything, he loved it when Coach Howie gave *him* a thumbs-up. Lately, Tom felt like everything he did was thumbs-down.

"What's up?" Harty gave Tom a friendly nudge.

"All this talk about superstitions and lucky goals makes me remember that I've lost my luck." Tom sighed. "I have . . . no lucky food, no lucky way to get dressed, no lucky socks, cap or Band-Aids. What kind of hockey player am I?"

"Oh, yeah," agreed Stuart. "Ask anyone. The best hockey players in the world have good luck charms. So do their fans and coaches."

The more Tom heard, the worse he felt. "I haven't scored a goal since last season, when I wore my old number 15 jersey. I used to say 'Go, Hawks, go!' as I pulled it over my head." Tom grunted in frustration. "This year I got dumb number 5. When we moved up to Team Three, my number 15 jersey stayed behind. Why can't Team Three have a number 15?"

"Glenlake teams don't have every number in the world," mumbled Jordan. "If they did,

I'd take number 32 like Jonathan Quick."

"I like number 66," said Harty.

"Remember what Coach Howie told us? Don't put hockey skates without skate guards in your hockey bag." Stuart shivered. "Maybe some kid's blades slashed that jersey to shreds."

Tom bent over to reach into his bag. *Ripppp!* His padded hockey pants split open. When he stood up, he bumped his head. "Oh, boy!" grumbled Tom. "Besides losing my good luck, I have found bad luck!"

Mark did not laugh. He looked at Tom as if to say, "You're right! You've got big time bad luck!"

The boys pulled their big hockey bags down the long hallway beneath the bleachers. They stopped by the spectator glass and checked out the new game on the ice. Novice Four teams were playing. Tom's eyes quickly picked out Glenlake number 15. "Hey, that girl is wearing my old jersey!" Tom watched the play. Number 15 blazed the ice, stickhandled the puck like a pro,

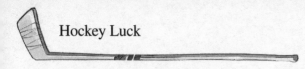

and then swooped to the right of the goalie and hammered a shot into the net. Goal!

Tom's heart sank. His old jersey had just worked its magic!

Sharing Luck

Mark gawked. "Man, oh man! Number 15 *is* a lucky jersey! Now that girl's got your luck! She's got *your* wicked slapshot, and she's scoring *your* goals." Mark patted Tom's shoulder. "Bummer. 'Cause you don't jive . . . wearing number 5!"

The truth was painful for Tom. He yanked his hockey bag. One wheel fell off. He dragged himself and his broken bag through the doorway.

"Tom! Over here!" shouted his mom,

waiting with the other parents near the snack bar. "Hurry up!" She tightened her yellow and green scarf.

Tom looked around. All Hawks parents, grandparents and fans were wearing the team colours. All for good luck and team spirit. Everybody had helped the Hawks win, except him.

Tom carried his bag down the front stairs and into the parking lot. His friends walked a few steps behind, whispering.

Just before getting into his car, Harty called out, "Hey, guys . . . how about road hockey at my house! Three o'clock!"

"Okay," said Tom, brightening. He loved road hockey almost as much as ice hockey. And there were no jerseys for road hockey, and no numbers. He'd get a goal for sure. No problem.

— • —

It was after three o'clock. Tom stick-handled a tennis ball down his driveway and along the sidewalk toward Harty's house. *TAP*, *TAP*, *TAP*. He concentrated on keeping his head up and grip loose. He looked ahead, pretending the light pole was the goal. He took a shot. *SWOOSH!* The ball missed the pole and bounced along the curb — *BOING*, *BOING*,

BOING — stopping beneath Mrs. Corbet's car. *What next?*

Tom shouldered his stick and picked up his pace.

A hockey net was set up and ready on Harty's driveway, but Tom's friends were nowhere in sight. *Did they say two o'clock*

or three o'clock? Did I miss the game?
worried Tom.

As Tom neared, he could see Harty's
garage door was open. His four friends were
sitting at a round table. It looked like they
were writing a spelling test. "We're in here!"
called Harty.

"What's up?" Tom scrunched his face,
feeling clued out.

"We are a team and we have a team
problem," said Jordan in a nervous robot
voice.

"Huh?" said Tom. His friends were acting
weird. They made him feel like he was
inside the principal's office.

Mark looked at the floor and spoke
quickly, "You got the most goals last year.

But this season . . . you are in a slump. And a funk. You need to dump the slump and fix the funk. And we are going to help you!" He let out a big breath. "Phew. I'm done."

Tom's face reddened. He knew how rotten his hockey was, but it didn't feel good to be insulted.

Mark jabbed Stuart and whispered, "Your turn."

"Tom. Um . . . First of all, you need some luck," Stuart said sincerely. "I'm used to tripping and crashing into stuff. But, that's not you! You are our star. The team counts on your goals."

"You are the guy who usually helps us!" said Harty. "Now it's our turn to help you."

The four friends put their fists together and yelled, "Tom's the best!"

Tom's spirits lifted. His friends were trying their hardest. He wondered, *Can my friends really help me become lucky again?*

"We have a plan," said Harty.

Stuart passed Tom an NHL Band-Aid. "I'm sharing my secret weapons with you."

Mark pulled a handful of mushroom pizza out of his pocket. "It's a bit mushy, but it's still a goal-getter. Just eat it and see!"

Jordan held out a bag full of broccoli. "You can grow stinky socks quickly if you stuff these into the sock toes."

Tom said, "Thanks, guys." But he was still concerned. "Luck doesn't come easily."

Harty held up his mom's tablet. "I've got

something that might help." Harty opened the cover. "I usually use this to look up the big words my mom uses. But we have something BIGGER to look up today! Like . . . what the NHL pros do for good luck." Harty touched the screen, concentrating on typing the words "NHL lucky charms" into the search bar.

"Okay," said Tom. He crossed his fingers. Maybe, just maybe, his friends and the entire NHL could help him find something to improve his luck.

NHL Luck

"Listen to this," said Harty, as he moved his fingers up and down the screen. "A good luck charm is 'something believed to bring good luck.'"

"Like, duh?" said Mark. "We need to know what the SOMETHING is! Like, if you paint your toenails on game day, you'll have powerful luck." He stomped his foot. "That's the kind of simple answer we're looking for!"

Stuart typed new words into the search

bar: "NHL hockey superstitions." Within seconds, a list appeared.

Mark tapped on the first answer. "The Detroit Red Wings' fans throw octopuses onto the ice for good luck!"

"Cool!" they chorused, flailing their arms like a wiggly octopus.

"The Florida Panthers' fans have thrown rats on the ice in hopes of getting a *rat trick*!" Stuart read. "I hate rats."

"Those superstitions are no good for Tom. He's a Hawk on the ice, not a fan in the stands!" said Mark. "What else?"

The tablet was passed around.

"I found a good one," said Harty. "NHL forward Bruce Gardiner used to dunk his stick in the toilet, wanting to show the stick who the boss was. He gave it a good flushing." Harty's eyes widened. "We've got a bathroom just inside the door. Let's go!"

Tom grabbed his stick. The boys headed to the bathroom, sounding like a bunch of owls. "Oooo." "Oooo." "Oooo." "This is going to be goooood!"

"Now, put the blade in the water!" Harty said to Tom, pointing to the bowl.

"Then swish it around!" said Jordan. "You are the boss! You rule!"

Tom followed along.

Stuart pressed down on the flush handle. *FLUSHHH!* The water swirled up to the toilet brim and then circled down the bowl and into the drain.

"Yes!" gasped the boys. "Cool!"

Harty's sister, Wendy, crept up behind Tom. "I'm telling my mom and you are in big trouble!" she exclaimed. "MO-OM! Tom is breaking our toilet! Come quick!"

Instantly, Harty's mom appeared. She stood in the doorway, arms crossed. "What on earth are you guys doing? Get that stick out of my toilet right now! If you want to play in the toilet, I will give you each a pair of rubber gloves and a cleaning brush!"

Tom's jaw was hanging open as they ran back to the garage. "I thought I was a dead duck," he cried.

"What now?" asked Stuart.

"Sidney Crosby eats a peanut butter and jelly sandwich before his games," said Harty. "I can make you one."

"Whoa! I don't like jelly," sighed Tom.

Mark scratched his head and grabbed the tablet. He searched more websites. "I found another good one!" he said. "There was a New York Ranger known as Gratoony the Loony who used to stand on his head before a game." Mark raised his eyebrows at Tom. "Wanna try it?"

Tom nodded in desperation.

Stuart organized a pile of sleeping bags, life jackets and tarps against the garage wall. "These will be your crash pad . . . just in case. SAFETY FIRST!"

Tom squatted down. He put his hands on the floor and his head between his hands. Harty and Jordan helped pull Tom's feet and legs up.

"No! No! I'm going to fall!" cried Tom. Jordan and Harty quickly pulled him into a handstand. "Ouch! My hands! My head! My back! Ouch! Oooo. Eyeee. Aaahooooh!"

"You should put Tom down," Stuart said. *"His face is purple."*

THUMP! Tom flopped onto the crash pads. "Aaahoooh!" he gave one last howl.

"What's going on in there?" yelled Harty's mom, hearing the commotion. "There will be *consequences* if you break something!"

"Told you about the big words. Let's play road hockey," said Harty, waving his friends outside.

Testing Luck

Tom's pockets were filled with broccoli and pizza. He stuck the NHL Band-Aid across his chin. "I'm ready to test my luck with this stuff!" Tom gave a goofy grin, fastened his helmet and then tripped on Stuart's foot. He slowly got to his feet.

The plastic puck passed from player to player. Forward, back and across the driveway. Jordan crouched in net, making his scary goalie face. *BAM! BAM! BAM!* Jordan stopped shot after shot. Tom went

for the rebound each time, and each time
he missed.

Tom made perfect stick-to-stick passes,
allowing Harty to score twice.

Five minutes later, Tom picked up a pass
from Mark. He ran down the left side of the
driveway, on a breakaway. *I got it. This is
it*, thought Tom, eyeing Jordan, blocking the
left. Tom took a shot, high and right. Jordan
stopped the puck with his goalie glove.

Stuart swooped in for the rebound. He
gently tapped the puck. It skipped between
Jordan's big leg pads. "Goal!" squealed
Stuart, dancing.

Tom dragged his feet. "How'd you do
that?"

"Got lucky," said Stuart.

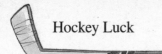

"*Shhh!*" Harty made a face at Stuart.

"Sorry, Tom. I forgot. I'm not supposed to mention our good luck to you," said Stuart. "It only makes you feel worse. But . . . the fact is . . . Jordan is the best goalie in the world, wearing the stinkiest socks in the world. That is why you can't score. You don't have a chance. I usually can't score, but my NHL Band-Aids are extremely lucky."

Tom pointed to the NHL Band-Aid on his chin. "This is not lucky . . . on me! Pizza in my pocket didn't work either. And the headstand gave me a sore neck."

"You want me to take off my socks?" asked Jordan. "You can try them."

"No!" gasped Tom, choking at the suggestion.

Jordan clapped. "I've got one more idea. Start talking to the net. That's what Patrick Roy, the goalie, did during NHL games."

Tom's hopes were fading. *Is it time to give up?* he wondered. But his friends continued to look optimistic.

"Be firm!" "You're the boss!" "You rule!" they coached.

Tom took in a big breath. *No! I am not a quitter. No one likes a quitter.* He held the orange plastic puck in his hand. In a stern voice, he said, "Listen up, net. This puck is going to hit you like a bullet, so get ready. I am getting the next goal today! Got it?"

"Good!" raved Harty.

"Now tap the posts with your stick," said Jordan.

Tom tapped the posts three times. He showed them who the boss was. Then he kissed the puck and said nicely, "Come on, plastic puck, be my buddy. Let's get a goal, just you and me."

But Tom did not score. He tripped over a tree branch and lost his shoe in a bush.

Tom plodded home. He'd had enough bad hockey for one day.

Back to Basics

It was Monday morning. The schoolyard was in chaos. Tom met his friends by the swings.

"I had nightmares all night," Tom told them. "Unlucky 5s were everywhere. The Hawks got five five-minute penalties. We got five goals against us. We had five players away. I got a nickel for my allowance. And I had a toothache! It was my worst nightmare yet."

"Yeah," said Mark. "I had a nightmare, too. Your bad luck rubbed off on us."

"No way," said Tom. But, he was worried. *What if my bad luck is contagious?* It was time to try something different.

"Coach Howie always says, 'Stick to the basics. Go back to square one if you are stuck in a rut.' Maybe it's time to go back to old-fashioned superstitions," suggested Tom.

The boys began to shout out every superstition they'd ever heard. "Don't step on a sidewalk crack!" "Don't let a black cat cross your path." "Cross your fingers." "Cross your toes." "Get a horseshoe." "Pinch yourself." "Find a four-leaf clover." "Find a penny, pick it up . . ."

"Canada doesn't have pennies anymore," said Tom.

"I bet our old teacher, Mrs. Wong, has one. She has everything," said Jordan.

The boys ran to her classroom door and knocked on it.

Mrs. Wong was putting up a bulletin board display for Thanksgiving. "Hello there!" she said, greeting them with a smile. "I really miss you guys. How are the Hawks doing?"

"Tom has lost his luck in hockey. It all started when he got his new jersey," said Stuart, "and lost his lucky number 15."

"Oh dear," said Mrs. Wong, shaking her head. "Hockey players have many superstitions. I remember when my brother said the word *shutout* before a big game. His team lost 9–0. I think he talked himself out of winning! He thought they'd lose and they did." She continued, "Then he kissed the Stanley Cup when it was at the public library, and his team won their next game!"

"Wow!" exclaimed Tom.

"Do you have a lucky penny?" asked Mark. "Tom could *kiss* it for good luck!"

"Good thinking! But I haven't found a lucky penny in a long time," sighed Mrs. Wong.

The boys looked deflated.

"Hmm . . . Let's just think," suggested Mrs. Wong, walking toward her desk.

She opened the bottom drawer and fished out an old calendar. "Here, Tom. Remember when we studied English proverbs and wise sayings? I was lucky to find 365 of them in this calendar! Proverbs are full of advice. Maybe you'll find one about good fortune and luck."

Tom liked Mrs. Wong. He missed having her as his teacher, even though he liked his new teacher, Miss Lucy.

BUZZZ! BUZZZ! The nine o'clock bell blasted.

"Don't be late for class!" said Mrs. Wong. "Remember . . . most of the time, we make our own luck!"

"Thank you," said Tom, waving goodbye. He hurried toward room number seven, carefully carrying 365 proverbs.

Making Lists

"Good morning, student geniuses," said Miss Lucy. She liked to call them important names. "Today you have a fun writing assignment! It will give you a chance to share something you know lots about." Miss Lucy hummed as she wrote the assignment on the board:

Write a list.
The title should start with:
"HOW TO_____"

Tom scratched his head. The only thing he liked to write about was hockey. "Does anyone want to share their idea?" asked Miss Lucy.

Jordan scuffed his feet under his desk.

"I'm going to write 'How to have a lemonade stand,'" said Laura. "There are lots of things to do, like make lemonade, get cups and paint a sign."

"I'm going to write 'How to become an author,'" said Kylie. "There are three easy steps."

"Excellent," said Miss Lucy. "You *can* do it, people! I smell brilliance in this classroom!" Miss Lucy had a way of making everything seem possible and everyone feel smart. "Go brains, go!" she cheered. "See if

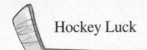

you can get twenty things on your list!"

Tom kept thinking. *I can't write "How to score a goal" because . . . I don't score any more! I HAVE BAD HOCKEY LUCK!* He held the calendar from Mrs. Wong. He opened it and read:

"Birds of a feather flock together." Tom nodded.

"Practice makes perfect." Tom nodded.

"The best way to have good luck is to stay away from bad luck."

Tom couldn't believe it. Even the calendar knew about hockey and how to solve luck problems. Suddenly, the proverb gave Tom an idea. He opened his journal and wrote:

How to have BAD hockey luck

1. Wear number 5 on your jersey.

2. Do not practise.

3. Be late.

4. Don't listen to your coach.

5. Fool around.

6. Eat lots of candy.

7. Be tired.

8. Forget your skates.

9. Forget to sharpen your skates.

10. Go to the wrong arena.

11. Forget your mouthguard.

12. Do not follow the rules.

13. Be crabby.

14. Make fun of your team.

15. Never say thank you to the parent helpers and coach.

16. Lose your lucky number . . . (especially to a girl who wears pink ribbons).

17. Be weird.

18. Pick your nose.

19. Bring your pet snake to the game.

20. Wear number 5 on your jersey!!!!!!!

Tom read his list. It was a beauty. It made him smile inside.

Miss Lucy strolled around the classroom telling kids how amazing they were. Even Jordan, who hated writing, was busy writing a long list: "How to build an outdoor rink."

Tom thought about his week. It didn't feel good to be crabby. He picked up his pencil and wrote a new journal entry. This one was easy peasy.

How to have GOOD hockey luck

1. Listen to your coach.

2. Practise.

3. Eat healthy food.

4. Be on time.

5. Drink water.

6. Get a good night's sleep.

7. Check your equipment bag so you don't forget your gear.

8. Get your skates sharpened.

9. Go to the correct arena.

10. Check the schedule!

11. Wear your mouthguard.

12. Follow the rules.

13. Be a team player.

14. Be happy!

15. Thank the coach and parent helpers.

16. Brush your teeth.

17. Don't pick your nose.

18. Leave your pet snake at home.

19. If you have to wear a number 5 jersey, try your best anyway.

20. Stay positive . . . (even if a girl with pink ribbons gets to wear your lucky number 15 jersey).

Tom thought about Mrs. Wong's words: "You make your own luck." Sometimes she had weird ideas. But the proverb calendar was a good idea today. Tom read it one more time, this time with a few extra words:

"The best way to have good hockey luck is to stay away from bad hockey luck."

Hard Work

On Tuesday morning, Tom sat at the kitchen table finishing spelling homework. Mom rushed back and forth making breakfast and doing laundry while Dad packed lunches. The toast burned, the coffee spilled and the smoke detector went off.

"Ewww!" Mom scowled as she picked something gooey out of Tom's jeans pocket. "This is disgusting!"

"That's Mark's lucky hockey pizza," said Tom. "I was supposed to eat it to improve my hockey luck."

Mom rolled her eyes. "That Mark is a real joker."

"No, Mom. When Mark eats pizza on game day, he scores a goal," said Tom. "Don't you believe in hockey superstitions?"

"Well . . . the scientist in me says, NO! Superstitions are ridiculous. If Mark got a goal, it's because he deserved it, not because he downed a pizza," Mom said.

Tom frowned. "But . . . but . . . Dad has hockey superstitions. He didn't shave and the Flames won!"

Mom sighed, "Well . . . I guess . . . some lucky charms might give you *hope.*

Some superstitions might make you *focus*. Having hope and focusing are good things. But you SHOULD NOT count on luck alone." She raised her finger. "Work hard and your luck will work!"

"I *have* been working hard at hockey," Tom sighed. "But I haven't scored a goal this season."

"Keep at it," said Dad. "Lazybones never find luck."

Phsshhh-splash-whoosh noises came from the washing machine, which was overflowing. Mom ran to hit the off button. "That's it!" She took off her blue sweater. "Every time I wear this thing, my day is a disaster!"

Dad whispered to Tom, "You'll know

when you find your luck. It will hit you like a red goal light."

——————•——————

It was an ordinary day at school. There was journal writing, two pages of math problems and a lesson about the Bow River. Mark yawned most of the afternoon. Then he made a big discovery. If you add the letter K to Miss Lucy's name, it becomes

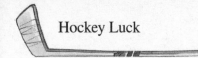

Miss Lucky. He passed Tom a note to tell him.

Miss Lucy stood by Tom's desk. She could read the note over Tom's shoulder.

Tom shuddered. Luckily, Miss Lucy didn't get mad. Instead she said, "How's your hockey luck doing?"

"Not good," Tom mumbled. He hadn't scored at recess when playing ball hockey. Every time he passed the ball, it ended up a goal for someone else. "All the kids are good at ball hockey now, so I need to be better."

"I liked your writing assignment about hockey luck," said Miss Lucy. "Hang in there!"

"Thanks," said Tom. Miss Lucy was nice.

Kylie sat across from Tom. She leaned

over and said, "If you want to be lucky, you need to be Irish. I can teach you an Irish jig."

Tom choked.

"Or an Irish sword dance," said Kylie.

"Hey, Tom," said Mark, making a face. "Swords are cool. But you might have to wear a green leprechaun suit to have the luck of the Irish."

"Get a grip! Hockey players don't wear leprechaun suits," groaned Jordan, rolling his eyes. "They wear padded pants."

Passing
the Puck

School was over. Tom grabbed his backpack and headed for the crosswalk. His dad was waiting for him in his truck, parked by the lane.

"Over here!" yelled Dad, waving a box of doughnut holes. Tom ran to meet him.

"Let's go to the hockey store," said Dad. "I tried to fix the rip in your hockey pants, but it was impossible. Duct tape won't stick. And I jammed up the sewing machine with black thread. Those pants are worn out and too small anyway." Dad smiled. "Time to buy you some new ones."

"Yes!" cheered Tom, downing a doughnut hole. *New pants!* His old ones were bought at a garage sale.

Dad tuned in the local *Hockey Talk* program on the car radio.

"Today we are talking about how lucky our city is to have Junior A hockey players who might be good enough to get university scholarships, play in the WHL or even the NHL. Our telephone lines are open," said the radio host. "Let's talk about it . . . "

"Maybe one day you will make the Mustangs' Junior A team," said Dad. "Get a scholarship and play in the NHL."

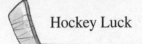

Wow! thought Tom. *Dad dreams big.* Then he remembered: *That's my dream, too!*

———— ● ————

The bright store buzzed with hockey players and parents shopping for gear. Tom and Dad checked out the skates on their way to the pants. "These will be next," said Dad. "You're growing like a weed!"

Tom tried on pants. The first pair was too padded. He looked like he had swallowed pillows. The next pair was too long. He couldn't bend his knees. The third pair was too big in the waist. They nearly fell to the floor as Tom stepped out of the change room.

Tom tried on the last pair. "This is it," he said.

"Walk around," suggested Dad. "Do some of your moves to make sure they're perfect. I'm going to find a helmet for me."

Tom sprang into action. He lunged, squatted, bent, reached and sat . . . next to a big guy wearing a Calgary Mustangs Junior A jacket. The name Baxter was on his arm.

Wow! I'm sitting next to Butch Baxter! He is the best forward in the league! thought Tom, nearly jumping out of his new pants. *The radio announcer just said he's going to the WHL draft!*

Butch Baxter was busy taping his new hockey stick. He wrapped the white tape around and around the blade, while muttering the alphabet. "A, B, C, D, E . . ." Finally, he looked at Tom. "You getting some new hockey pants?"

"Yes. My old ones ripped," said Tom.

"Hope you got a goal when they ripped," said Butch.

"Nope," said Tom, nervously. His cheeks burned. How could he tell Butch Baxter that he didn't score goals? That his pants ripped in the dressing room?

"Oops. Sorry, dude," said Butch, looking at Tom's embarrassed face. "I only got a few goals last season! Just didn't happen with all the good goalies out there."

"But . . . but . . . you're the best forward," said Tom, with admiration. "Everyone says that!"

"That's because I pass the puck and *assist* the goals. I play as part of a team, not as a puck hog. Puck hogs are players who only go for goals. And when the other team figures it out, they go after *him*."

Tom listened hard.

Butch continued, "It takes more than one player to score. Everyone has a job on the ice. I try to line up the puck so that the best-positioned player can fire it into the net. Sometimes it's me, and sometimes it's not." Butch smiled. "And I'm lucky to have good defence behind me. They keep the puck away from our goal and feed it to me." Butch taped a few more loops. "I got the record for most assists last season: 105. And 5 assists in one game!" He pointed at

Tom. "You get any assists yet?"

"Yeah . . . all the time. I already got seven assists this season, and we've only played six games!" said Tom.

"Good job. That's golden!" Butch gave Tom a thumbs-up.

Suddenly Tom felt like a million bucks. All along, he hadn't let his team down. And . . . he'd never known assists were that important.

Butch checked the time on his phone. "It's time to get to the arena. I *ALWAYS* tape my socks at exactly two hours and eight minutes before a game. That's when I get into the zone and give myself a pep talk."

"What zone?" Tom asked.

"My zone. It's when I concentrate and

focus on my game. I get my mind prepared to play," said Butch. "Your *brain* and *body* need to be ready for a big game."

"Oh," squeaked Tom. He'd never thought of that either.

"Keep on passing!" said Butch. "Remember: a team wins together and loses together!"

"Okay, I'll keep passing," Tom assured Butch. But as Tom sat on the bench waiting for Dad, he had another thought. He crossed his fingers and said, "I'd like . . . just one more goal."

Lucky Tape

The house smelled like spicy spaghetti sauce. Tom put on his new hockey pants to show Mom.

"Nice," she said, turning him around. "Sturdy. Safe. Hey, what's this?" Mom peeled off a piece of stick tape stuck to Tom's backside. It was the length of a hot dog.

"Wowzers! That's from Butch Baxter! From when he taped his stick at the hockey store!" Tom hung the tape from his thumb. "It looks exactly like a . . . number 1!"

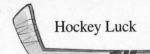

Suddenly he had a mega idea.

Tom bolted to the mud room. His hockey bag sat open on the floor. He dug out his white home jersey. He put it on the floor, the large number on the back facing him. "Goodbye, number 5!" he said, sticking the number 1 beside the number 5. The white tape was almost invisible on the white jersey, but Tom knew it was there. "YES!" The piece of tape made his new jersey into an old secret weapon . . . number 15!

"Go, Hawks, go!" said Tom, as he pulled the jersey over his head. He ran to the backyard, grabbing his stick and a bucket of pucks on the way.

Old tires leaned against the brick wall. Tom used to be good at shooting pucks into the middle of the tires. He had done it hundreds of times. Now it was time to test his number 15.

Let's go! Tom fired a quick wrist shot, hitting the target on his first try.

"Bull's eye!" Tom shouted. "I'm back!" He almost cried happy tears.

Tom fired shot after shot, hitting the target almost every time. Then he thought about what Butch Baxter told him. *A great hockey player makes good passes. A team wins together and loses together.* Tom wondered how he could practise his passing.

Soon Tom had a new idea. He grabbed a tennis ball and hit it against the brick wall. The rebound was like a pass back to him. Tom picked up the ball on his stick, over and over, like a pass-receive drill. It wasn't perfect, but it felt great to keep the ball moving. When the ball was near the last target, Tom took a shot . . . and scored!

Mom came out of the house. "Tom, look at you! You have that hockey sweat head going on."

Tom glowed. Sweat head felt amazing!

"Now come inside for dinner. And *PEE-YEW!* Take off that smelly jersey. I'd better wash it for your game tomorrow," said Mom, rushing back to the kitchen.

Oh, no. Tom quivered. *Not number 15!* He took off the jersey and hid it inside his hockey helmet.

A rush of excitement tingled over Tom. Number 15 was going to surprise everyone!

Secret Luck

Wednesday.

Tom walked to school, still dreaming about hitting the tire targets in his backyard. He spied his friends and rushed to meet them. "Hey, guys! I'm here!"

"It's game day!" exclaimed Harty. "I've already checked my hockey gear."

"I'm ready, too!" said Jordan. He was wearing stinky socks.

Mark licked his lips. "I have Hawaiian pizza for recess snack and slapshot salami pizza for lunch."

Stuart looked worried. "I'm wearing my last NHL Band-Aid. Hope it doesn't fall off."

Tom whistled and hummed, nearly dancing an Irish jig. He had something lucky, too.

His friends raised their eyebrows at him. "What's going on?" they asked.

"Your smile is as big as a banana," said Mark.

Oh, no. Tom gulped. More than anything, he wanted to tell them about number 15 and how his luck was back. But Tom worried about bragging. If he shared his secret weapon, would it still be a secret? But mostly, would it still work?

Tom thought quickly, then said, "Coach

Howie said we need a *positive* attitude. I am positive that we are going to have a good game!" He knocked his knuckles on his head and said, "Touch wood!"

"TOUCH WOOD!" they repeated, rapping heads.

The school day whizzed by. Tom doodled lucky 15s in every notebook.

— ● —

It was exactly two hours and eight minutes before game time. Tom ate a bowl of hamburger soup. He checked his hockey bag. Everything was there.

"Where's Mom?" Tom asked.

"At work," answered Dad, without looking up from his laptop.

"But, it's game day!" said Tom. *What if we're late?* He remembered his "How to have bad hockey luck" and his "How to have good hockey luck" lists.

Tom checked the schedule. "Dad! Our game is at Crowfoot Arena. That's in Northwest Calgary."

Dad stopped. "Wow! That was lucky you checked. I assumed the game was at Centennial Arena since you're the home team. I'd better phone Mom."

Tom and Dad hurried. They picked up Jordan and headed up Crowchild Trail to the arena. The car was quiet. Dad concentrated on the traffic. Tom and Jordan stared out the windows. They were concentrating, too.

Tom visualized himself skating down the ice, grabbing a pass and shooting it along the boards. He picked up the puck, passed and then positioned himself by the net. Should he shoot or pass?

"There's Mom," said Dad, pulling into the parking lot. She waved her yellow and green gloves.

"Our friends are here," said Tom, recognizing Mark's van. It had a Calgary Flames car flag sticking up from the window.

Coach Howie carried a first aid kit, coach's binder and a bucket of practice pucks up the stairs. He greeted the coach from the Falcons.

"Yeah! Let's go!" cheered Tom, ready to work hard for his team, the Hawks.

In the Zone

The dressing room rocked. The Hawks were *getting into the zone* with special routines. Everyone did something different. There was toe touching, knuckle cracking, hair combing, sock taping and music playing. Lucky charms sat on the bench: a superhero action figure, a lucky tape-ball, NHL playing cards, a bag of black rocks and a stuffed toy hawk.

Harty carefully put on his gear, paying attention to the lucky order. Elbow pads first, jock second . . .

Jordan's socks stank.

Mark patted his stomach, full of pizza.

Stuart wrote the letters NHL onto beige Band-Aids, using a black felt marker. He stuck them on his arm. "I've invented my own lucky Band-Aids," he said, "because I ran out of the real ones."

Tom suited up, saving the best for last. He slipped the number 15 jersey out of his bag without letting the team see the piece of stick tape. "Go, Hawks, go!" he said, poking his head through the neck hole.

Tom leaned back against the wall, making sure no one saw the tape. He felt the luck of 15 run up and down his back. A smile spread across his face. This was going to be his lucky day!

Coach Howie gave a quick pep talk. "Let's get out on the ice and play our best. We are not loony birds making nonsense plays . . . we are . . ."

"HAWKS!" shouted the team.

Tom fastened his helmet, sucked in a big breath of courage and thought, *Let's go, number 15*. He grabbed his stick, keeping his back close to the wall, and positioned himself at the end of the line.

The team filed out the door, along the mat and onto the ice. As Tom looked up into the stands, he could see his mom, dad, grandparents and all the Hawks' fans. They were wearing yellow and green. Everyone cheered, "Go Hawks!"

"Break a leg!" shouted Harty's sister, Wendy.

"What?" Stuart panicked. "That's horrible! I don't want to break my leg!"

"Me neither," agreed Tom.

"It's a saying that means good luck. People say it before actors or dancers go on stage," said Harty, defending Wendy.

"How about we *break a sweat?*" said Tom. "We have five minutes to warm up."

Tom dug his blades into the ice and pushed off with long, smooth strides. He cruised by the players' bench and penalty box. No penalties! he reminded himself. He skated around the corners, doing perfect crossovers. He did a lap skating backwards, then stopped and joined a group taking shots on net.

Bang! Bang! Bang! Jordan stopped shot after shot. But he missed a five-hole, when Tom slid one through his open legs.

"Goal!" Tom squealed, losing his breath. "I got a goal!" He danced about like a guy with ants in his new hockey pants. *Number 15 is magic!* he told himself. Now his muscles were warm, and he was filled with confidence and luck!

Tom's friends started howling.

"Wow!"

"Wicked!"

"High-ten!"

"That's pizza perfect!"

The team gathered in front of their bench with Coach Howie, ready for their cheer. "Hawks!" they yelled, at the top of their lungs.

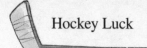

Tom skated to centre ice and set up for the faceoff . . . with a big smile on his face.

Game On

Plonk! The referee dropped the puck.

Tom swiped his stick, catching the puck and sending it to Mark on right wing. Mark skated along the boards and sailed the puck back to Tom. Tom skated hard to pick up the pass, but a Falcon barrelled ahead, grabbing the puck with his blade.

The Falcon raced down the ice, with Tom and Mark chasing after him. Stuart skated backwards, forcing the Falcon to the side, away from the goal. Jordan positioned himself and made his ugly goalie face. *Grrmph!* The Falcon took a shot. He missed!

Stuart swooped in and grabbed the rebound. He quickly skated behind the net. He caught Tom's eyes and passed the puck right onto Tom's stick.

Tom skated up the middle of the ice. He passed to Mark. Mark returned the pass to Tom. Tom passed to Harty. Harty smacked the puck . . . right into the Falcons' net! GOAL!

"Yay!" shouted Tom, slapping high-fives with his friends.

"Yay!" screamed the players on the bench.

"Yay, Hawks!" the fans cheered. They waved their yellow and green flags.

Tom felt good skating to the bench. He heard the referee tell the scorekeepers, "Goal by number 8, assisted by number 5." Tom knew it was his number 15 bringing him good hockey luck. He watched the scoreboard post the goal: 1–0 for the Hawks.

A few minutes later, the Falcons had the puck. Their left winger skated around the Hawks and passed to an open player. She wound up at the blue line and pounded a slapshot right over Jordan's shoulder. GOAL! Now the score was 1–1.

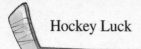
"Rats," sighed Tom.

Jordan swigged back a drink of water. He shook his foot.

By the middle of the second period, the Hawks were in trouble. The score was 3–1 for the Falcons. The puck was in the Hawks' end. Tom felt sick inside.

"C'mon, 15. C'mon, 15." Tom begged for more luck. He stepped onto the ice to take the faceoff. "I can do it. I can do it."

Jordan scolded his skates as he stomped his feet. It looked like he was trying to wake up his stinky socks. As Tom skated by him, he said, "Hang in there, buddy!"

Jordan nodded and crouched into position.

"Go, Hawks, go! Go, Hawks, go!" chanted the fans.

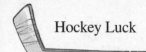
Tom ignored the crowd. He ignored the score. He focused. The puck dropped.

Tom won the faceoff, making a slick pass to Mark. Mark skated down the ice. The puck zigzagged from Mark to Tom to Mark. Mark fired a shot. He scored!

"Yahoo!" hollered Tom.

"Yay!" cheered the fans.

"Yay!" The team banged their sticks on the boards.

The referee announced, "Goal by number 18, assisted by number 5."

Remembering what Butch Baxter said about assists made Tom glow.

The scoreboard read 3–2 for the Falcons.

The game continued at a fast pace. Coach Howie switched players on the ice every few minutes. He called for a time out.

"Keep up the good work, Hawks," Coach Howie told the team. "No penalties. A Falcons power play would kill us right now."

The clock dropped to two minutes remaining.

Stay strong! Tom told himself, stepping out of the players' box. He hustled to the action, jabbed his stick out and stole the puck. Tom dug his skates into the ice and got a breakaway! Nobody could catch him. Using a quick wrist shot, Tom fired the puck under the goalie's gloved hand. Goal!

"Yes!" Tom raised his arms and jumped about like an Irish dancer doing a sword dance.

His friends huddled around. "Woo-hoo!" they whooped and high-fived.

Excitement swirled inside Tom as he looked up into the stands. His parents waved like crazy. His Grandma Dot rang her cowbell. *Clang! Clang! Clang!*

"Yay!" shouted the crowd.

BUZZZ! The time clock sounded. The game was over. The final score was 3–3.

The Hawks and Falcons met on the ice to shake hands.

"Good game!" the Falcons' coach told Tom as he passed by him.

"Good game," agreed Tom.

Teamwork

The dressing room filled with sweat-head Hawks, all fired up.

"Two assists and one goal! Wowzers!" Tom zinged. He knew he couldn't have done it without lucky 15 on his back.

Tom peeled off his wet jersey. "What?" He panicked. The piece of tape from Butch Baxter was gone. *WHAT?? Oh, NO!* He couldn't believe his eyes. All he saw was the number 5!

Quickly, Tom searched the dressing

room. As he walked toward the door, he saw the hot-dog length tape stuck to the wall.

There was only one time my back touched that wall, he remembered. *On the way out the door, BEFORE the game!*

Suddenly Tom had a brain flash, sparking like a red goal light. *Lucky 15 did NOT help me!* He staggered back to the bench in shock. *I played my best game this season with the worst luck . . . NUMBER 5!*

Coach Howie entered the dressing room carrying the game sheet. "Nice game, Hawks!" he hollered. He held up one hand.

They all sat up and listened.

"You worked hard out there," Coach Howie complimented them. "The game was fast. Our opposition was tough." He smiled.

"We had no fluky goals. No penalties. No excuses. The passing was crisp. The shift changes were slick." He gave a thumbs-up. "You used your skills and your brains! Good comeback! Good job, HAWKS!"

"Yay!" the Hawks shouted.

Tom liked Coach Howie. It felt good to make him proud.

Mark called out, "It looks like a bird bath in here!" He shook his head, sprinkling his sweat outward.

The room exploded with laughter. Sweat was flying everywhere.

"I thought we were dead ducks when it was 3–1!" Mark continued. "But we kept pecking at that puck. Put two more eggs in the nest . . ."

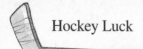

"Yeah!" Everyone laughed along.

"And . . ." Mark motioned his friends to

huddle together. He flicked his eyebrows and sang, "Tom's ALIVE . . . wearing number 5!"

"Yay, Tom!" Jordan waved a stinky sock in celebration.

Stuart shook his box of Band-Aids like a noisemaker. "Yippee!"

Harty gave Tom a high-ten. "That was top shelf!"

"Thanks, guys," said Tom, smiling ear to ear. "Teamwork got the goals and assists, not just me!"

Mark chomped down on a piece of cold pizza. "So, you find a lucky charm yet? Spill the beans, man!"

"No!" crowed Tom. "Guess I should keep looking for my hockey luck."

"We'll help you," said Stuart. "Count on us!"

Tom stopped and thought: *TEAMWORK is my lucky charm! Getting goals is easier when we work together.*

"Let's hurry!" said Jordan. "The Flames game will be on the car radio!"

Tom proudly stuffed his number 5 jersey into his hockey bag. He smiled even more. *I am so lucky to have four best friends. They make everything fun! AND . . . together we make FIVE.*

Meet the Glenlake Hawks

Tom Hiller

Jersey number: 5 and 15

Favourite position: Centre

Best hockey moment: All hockey moments are best for Tom.

Worst hockey moment: Drinking too much Lucky Lemon Guzzle before a tryout. It's difficult to skate fast when you have to pee.

Hockey superstition: Tom thinks his jersey brings him good luck.

Hobbies: Tom likes to play street hockey on his driveway, shinny at the outdoor rink in Crescent Park and ball hockey at recess. Before bed he reads books — about hockey.

Quotable quote: "I love hockey! I always try my best to be a good friend and a good team player."

Jordan Deerfoot

Jersey number: 1

Favourite position: Goalie

Best hockey moment: Stopping the puck from going into the net. Getting a shutout.

Worst hockey moment: Being late and keeping his carpool waiting. The team has only one goalie and without him, they can't play.

Hockey superstition: Jordan thinks his hockey socks bring him good luck. He hides them in his helmet so that they are never washed. The stinkier, the better.

Hobbies: Jordan likes to practise his goalie moves and scary goalie face with his older brother, Derek.

Quotable quote: "Try not to worry. When I get nervous, I get the jitters. Have fun no matter what."

Mark Boswell

Jersey number: 4

Favourite position: Right wing

Best hockey moment: Going to a real NHL game and dancing with the Calgary Flames mascot, Harvey the Hound.

Worst hockey moment: The day he forgot to bring his mouthguard to a big game. When he asked his teammates if he could borrow theirs, they wouldn't spit them out.

Hockey superstition: Mark thinks eating pizza before a game brings him good luck. His motto: Extra cheesy makes scoring easy!

Hobbies: Mark likes to think up funny jokes, riddles and poems. He often invents new team cheers.

Quotable quote: "It's great to laugh at a funny joke. But it's not great to laugh at your teammates when they are trying to be serious. Remember: your belly button will turn green if you are mean!"

Stuart Vickers

Jersey number: 11

Favourite position: Defence

Best hockey moment: Blocking a giant Black Bears player from scoring on the Hawks.

Worst hockey moment: Sometimes Stuart is clumsy. One time he forgot to take off his skate guards. When he stepped onto the ice, he tripped and fell, sending his open water bottle exploding through the air.

Hockey superstition: Stuart thinks he has good hockey luck when he wears Band-Aids with NHL team logos on them.

Hobbies: Playing at the outdoor rink in Crescent Park, across from his house. Stuart likes to use his walkie-talkie to call home and politely ask for hot chocolate for his friends.

Quotable quote: "Safety first! Always wear your helmet, pads, jock, neck guard and mouthguard!"

Harty McBey

Jersey number: 8

Favourite position: Centre

Best hockey moment: Scoring his first goal.

Worst hockey moment: When Harty moved to the Chinook Park neighbourhood he had to prove himself to a new team. It was hard to fit in at first.

Hockey superstition: Harty gets dressed in a special order for good luck. Then he tucks in the left side of his jersey — just like Wayne Gretzky did.

Hobbies: Harty likes to hang out at home, with his friends, in the garage. The walls are covered with NHL posters, the outdoor rink equipment is stored on the shelves, and there is an old slush machine to make yummy strawberry slush drinks.

Quotable quote: "Give your teammates a high-five! And if you cross your arms into an 'X,' you can give them a high-ten!"

Meet the Author

Irene Punt

Jersey number: I own a #66 Calgary Flames jersey. When I give presentations, I turn the jersey upside-down to show how it becomes #99. I secretly hope to write 99 books!

Favourite position: My favourite position is sitting at my laptop, writing more hockey books.

Best hockey moment: My two sons, Tom and Harty, played hockey in Calgary for the real Glenlake Hawks team, and my husband helped coach. My best hockey moments were seeing their amazing team spirit and good sportsmanship.

Worst hockey moment: One time I carpooled my boys and their friends to the wrong arena on game day. I found the correct arena just in time!

Hockey superstition: My best good luck charm is crossing my fingers. However, I also had a special game ritual when it looked like a landslide loss for the Hawks. I'd go get a cup of coffee at the concession. Often, as soon as I left the stands, the Hawks would score!

Hobbies: I like to ski, play badminton, golf, power walk, travel and hang out with my family and friends. I like to have fun and find new things to write about.

Quotable quote: "Thank you for reading my books! I love writing them!"

If Irene could say one more thing, what would it be? Writing a book is a team sport. My family helps me get the hockey scenes right. My first readers have given the raw manuscripts extra tweaks. My Scholastic team helps to polish them up. And the booksellers work hard to get the stories out to readers who love humour, action and hockey! Yay for TEAMWORK!

Irene Punt lives in Calgary, Alberta, with her husband and two sons. She spends a lot of time in Whitefish, Montana, and Nuevo Vallarta, Mexico. Before becoming an author she was a teacher. But she will always be a hockey mom.

Read more of Irene Punt's Glenlake Hawks books!

978-0-439-94897-5

The Wicked Slapshot

Tom isn't looking forward to hockey camp because his friends aren't going. But soon he's having fun doing the drills with his new friend Harty. Tom even invites Harty to his house for more practice and figures out a way to help him with his slapshot. Months later the two boys are surprised to find themselves playing against each other in a big tournament. Who will win?

978-0-545-99681-5

The Funny Faceoff

The Glenlake Hawks are having a great hockey season, on the ice and in the dressing room. Tom and his friends take some of their team spirit to the classroom and the schoolyard. But after a funny presentation in class goes a bit haywire, they are sent to the principal's office. Can the boys use hockey teamwork to save the day?

978-0-545-99765-2

Hockey Rules!

Tom is the envy of his friends. His teenage babysitter, Jeff, is totally cool — he even plays road hockey! — until he becomes a referee. Jeff the Ref gives Tom's team penalties and calls off goals! Things get out of hand when Tom and his friends decide to get back at Jeff. But after they accidentally send a mean email, Tom realizes it's much cooler to play by the rules.

978-1-4431-4649-4

Hockey Timeout

The Glenlake Hawks are gearing up for a big game against the Grey Wolves. Sam, the Hawks' top goal-scorer, might just be able to best the Wolves' superstar goalie. But when Sam's bad attitude and poor sportsmanship start affecting the rest of the team, can Tom get everyone back on track?